ANNA & BRONWYN
Priestesses of Avalon

MARNI L.B. TROOP & BECCA C. SMITH

Published by Red Frog Publishing a division of Red Frog Media

Visit our website at www.redfrogpublishing.com

First published in 2022

ISBN 9781949877458

Printed in the United States of America

Dedication

I dedicate it to my parents, who inspired my love of Arthurian legends and to my children, who are the sources of magic in my world.

- Marni L.B. Troop

To all the dreamers out there that believe in magic and pay it forward! This one is for you.

-Becca C. Smith

Chapter 1
ANNA

I despised Bronwyn.

How could anyone be so obnoxious and insolent and . . . just *rude*? Everyone fawned all over her as if she were High Priestess Florette herself. Why would anyone listen to a word she said?

Because she was powerful—more powerful than me—and it infuriated me to no end. I knew I was being petty and envious, but she could be so cruel. Not to anyone else on Avalon, but to me specifically. No matter what I said or did, Bronwyn would always demean me in front of the other priestesses-in-training. My life was infinitely better before she arrived two years ago. Most girls here were like me, given to Avalon to be fostered and trained at the age of seven. But Bronwyn? She was fourteen when she arrived! Fourteen! A prodigy, the priestesses informed us. Evidently, her small village was terrified of her because she couldn't control her immense powers. I had actually felt sorry for her, and in the beginning, I wanted desperately to be her friend. Something about her radiated charisma. But when she was assigned to me for tutoring, she had refused to listen to a word I said.

When I tried to show her how to incant a simple levitation spell, Bronwyn grew so angry that she used her innate magic against me by pushing me off my stool with her *mind*.

Using magic against other trainees was strictly forbidden in Avalon. I thought for sure High Priestess Elaine would banish her from the island immediately.

Not even close.

High Priestesses Elaine and Florette decided that the two of us needed to learn from each other and kept pairing us up as if we were friends who'd had a friendly spat.

Needless to say, the last two years had been one argument after another, making my life a miserable torment. I had friends before she arrived, but after a few weeks of constant bickering, everyone took her side, and it left me with no one.

Aside from High Priestesses Elaine and Florette, I didn't have anyone to talk to. Bronwyn had labeled me as a know-it-all, and it stuck. For good. I was completely alone. It hurt. Some nights I would cry myself to sleep. But I couldn't let Bronwyn see. I'd never let her have the satisfaction.

We couldn't be more opposite, both physically and mentally. She had long wavy black hair with dark eyes and an athletic build, whereas I had blue eyes, and my hair was stick straight and blond. I was also "too" skinny, according to the priestesses, even though I had a healthy appetite. The other priestesses-in-training used to make wagers on whether or not I could finish a whole pie in one sitting. One time I managed to scarf down High Priestess Elaine's apple pie in less time than it took to serve it. That was before Bronwyn, when I actually had friends.

2

My heart ached remembering what it was like to have a friend. I missed it. I missed having people to talk to.

At least I had the magic tomes in the Avalon library. They were my true joy, my true friends. Learning and memorizing incantations was the only thing that made my chest swell with happiness. Sometimes I would spend all night in the library without sleeping a wink. I'd be so involved in a book I wouldn't notice it was dawn. It was the perfect escape. I was good at it—better than anyone on Avalon, except for maybe High Priestess Florette. But I hoped to live up to her expectations someday. She meant the world to me and helped me in my darkest moments. Though I rarely saw her since she ruled over all of Avalon, the brief times I had spent with her were magical to me.

"Settle down, girls. We're working on scrying today," High Priestess Elaine announced to the class.

Our cozy classroom was a small space in the north corner of the Avalon fortress. The walls were made of thick, wide stone stacked in alternating, uneven rows. There was a fireplace in the back for cold winters, but since it was early summer, the coolness of the stone was refreshing. We used five long wooden tables for practicing spells and alchemy with pine benches for us to sit on.

Ten girls attended the session today, and we all wore the standard garb of an Avalon priestess-in-training: tan floor-length woolen dresses tied with a simple brown rope. Aside from the occasional itchy feeling, they were quite comfortable. The priestesses and high priestesses wore more elaborate robes, but only in fabric choice; the colors and style were all the same.

High Priestess Elaine stood at the front of the room, her pursed lips and narrowed eyes signaling her irritation at my fellow students' lack of attention.

3

And Bronwyn was at the forefront of the disturbers.

Which was why I was so infuriated. Elaine was one of my favorite people, and talking when she asked gently for silence was just . . . bad mannered. I was mad for her. So mad I couldn't seem to stop myself from saying, "She said be quiet!" My tone was harsh, but it felt surprisingly good to snap at Bronwyn and her lackeys.

Bronwyn shut her mouth, eyes judging. "Someone's trying to curry favor," she said.

"I'm simply being courteous: something you'd know nothing about," I snapped back. Why did I always take the bait? I hated myself for it as much as I disliked her. She brought the worst out in me, and what aggravated me more was the fact that *I* let her! No wonder I didn't have any friends. Who wanted to be friends with someone who constantly attacked the "golden child" of Avalon? Apparently, no one.

"Courteous?" Bronwyn guffawed. "That is the *last* word I'd use to describe you."

The entire class laughed with her.

I decided to keep my mouth closed and ignore Bronwyn. I didn't want any more reasons for the other girls not to like me. They despised me enough as it was.

And I *was* courteous, though apparently no one else thought so, which made me realize how the last two years had truly affected me.

Elaine stepped in and rescued me from any more humiliation. "Girls! That is enough! You are all training to be priestesses here in Avalon, so act like it and stop this petty bickering." She straightened her long, flowing robe. "Now. Where was I? Oh yes, scrying. You'll split into pairs of your choice, except for you, Anna and Bronwyn. You'll be partners for this session."

4

My shoulders slumped at her words. I didn't know who was more disappointed, me or Bronwyn. But it wasn't exactly a surprise. Elaine always paired us up after one of our sniping matches. She seemed to believe this would somehow bring us closer together, but it only made it worse. We were fated to dislike each other forever.

I walked over to where she sat since I knew she was too stubborn to come to me.

She rolled her eyes contemptuously. "Are you going to show me how you've already mastered the art of scrying?" Sarcasm dripped from every word.

I wanted to lie and say that I had, but I didn't know the first thing about scrying. It used innate magic like Bronwyn's. To make the scrying stone show its intended target took the magic from the user. I hadn't been able to tap into that part of me yet, and oftentimes young priestesses never would. A trainee's strength would fall into either of the two categories: incantation or soulbound. Bronwyn and I were as powerful as any trainees ever recorded, she with soulbound magic and I with incantation. If we actually liked each other, our powers combined would be unstoppable. It was probably why the priestesses kept placing us together.

But we couldn't be further apart.

Instead of answering her with attitude, I decided to be the bigger person and at least attempt to be civil. "Scrying is very difficult. I'm certain it will take me a while to understand it fully," I stated. I hated admitting my weaknesses to her, but arguing was exhausting. All I wanted to do was quietly learn how to scry without concern over what my next comeback would be.

To my shock, Bronwyn's face softened. "It's not that complicated. I can teach you a few tricks."

I stared at her, waiting for the attitude to come forth, but it didn't.

She handed me the stone. "It's all about concentration."

"It is all about concentration," High Priestess Elaine announced to the class.

I smiled at the echoed advice, and Bronwyn smiled back.

I didn't move. Was this a genuine moment we were having? Could we actually be finding common ground? Would our endless fighting finally end? I had to admit that the thought filled me with warmth. Disliking someone took a lot of energy, and I was tired of despising her.

I took the stone in my hands and closed my eyes, focusing on my favorite spot on Avalon Island. It was a small outcropping of trees overlooking a freshwater stream. It was my sanctuary when everything was too overwhelming to handle. The purpose of the stone was to show the user what they wanted to see. If I hadn't been scared of Bronwyn's reaction, I would have tried to take a gander at Khalid. He was a Moorish guard who helped keep Avalon safe, and he was beautiful. Of course, we had never spoken besides passing pleasantries. Guards mainly kept to themselves, taking their jobs very seriously. Besides, I was too shy, and what could I possibly say? *Hello, do you like your job? You're beautiful. I love you.* No. Not pathetic at all!

An eruption of laughter jolted me out of my daydream.

I opened my eyes, and an image of Khalid was in the scrying stone.

I dropped it on the table, and he disappeared.

Joanna McTirvish leaned in, still amused at my humiliation. "You *like* Khalid?" she asked loudly enough for the entire class to hear.

I didn't know what to say. I didn't know what to do, so I

6

reverted to my angry side. "It's none of your business who I like and who I don't like! Besides, I was focusing on . . ." *Where was he located?* I tried to remember the image on the stone before I had broken the connection, but I couldn't recall a thing! ". . . the building he was guarding," I said lamely.

The girls laughed harder.

"Settle down, priestesses, and focus on your lesson," Elaine said.

Joanna wasn't done. "Maybe we should tell him. Let him know that his true love lives right here on Avalon."

The others giggled.

If anyone told Khalid I liked him, I'd be mortified. "You wouldn't!" I exclaimed.

This only fueled Joanna's fire. "The expression on your face is proof enough for me. You're positively lovesick. Don't you think, Bronwyn?"

Glancing at Bronwyn, I hoped our brief truce would extend into defending me from Joanna and her big mouth.

Bronwyn's eyes moved from me to Joanna, then back again, as if she were debating what side she wanted to be on.

Predictably, she chose Joanna.

Bronwyn smiled. "Oh, I think Khalid in entitled to know who his admirers are." Though her words mocked me, the shift in her seat and darting eyes told me she was uncomfortable saying them. It was something.

But not enough for me.

I stood up and turned to High Priestess Elaine. "I'm feeling faint. May I be excused?"

"I know full well that you are not feeling anything of the sort." Elaine paused. "But you are free to go."

The other girls began to pack their things into knapsacks.

Elaine's tone turned severe. "I never said any of the rest of you could leave." She directed her gaze at me and whispered, "I think you have a young man to visit before these ladies can get to him first."

I was full of both relief and dread. She was right, of course. I had to find Khalid and tell him . . . something. Anything to keep him from hearing that I liked him. If he knew, he'd think I was one of the many young girls who followed him around and giggled whenever he gave them the time of day.

I took my knapsack and exited through the heavy wooden door that led to the rest of the fortress. I walked with purpose, traversing the stone hallways until I stood outside with the sun on my face.

Standing in front of the structure gave me a perfect view of Avalon Island. Stunning bright green rolling hills surrounded by richly colored pines, like arms embracing the island, spread out before me. Beyond the tree line, the vibrant blue waters sparkled in the beaming sunlight, and the golden sands stretched around the island, making up the shoreline.

The island itself was hidden in the mists in the very center of England. Only priestesses possessed the magic that could open a gateway to the mystical island. I was seven years old the first time I stepped foot on Avalon, and my parents had left me on the shore as I had climbed onto the skiff that would lead me to my new home. They had been so proud of me. No one in our family had ever been a priestess before, so to find the gift in me was both surprising and a source of fierce pride for my family. I hoped to see them again someday, but studying to be a priestess meant we had to cut all ties to the outside world. I missed my brother and my parents. Though

I was young when I left, I still remembered laughing and playing with them all.

High Priestess Florette was the one who had steered the small boat. I remembered when she waved her hand in the fog-filled air and incanted a few words. It was as if the mist sliced the air in half, creating an opening for us to pass through. I had been too amazed to even notice that the boat moved on its own without the need of an oarsman. It was just another part of the magic that was Avalon.

When we left the gray fog of England, the sky of the mystical island opened before us, and it was the deepest blue I had ever seen. I had stepped into another place, a place that was slightly out of time with the real world. It was what kept us protected from the outside. In the past, there had been other magic users or sovereigns who had wanted to attack us and control us for their own gain. But once the priestesses hid the island from space and time, we were safe from harm.

Stepping onto the pebble-strewn shore, I was greeted by the beauty of the green rolling hills and ancient pines. At the very top of the highest hill was the deep gray stone fortress of Avalon proper with its high walls and its towering turrets. It had taken my breath away.

Even with the other girls ostracizing me from a social life, I still loved this place. It made me feel safe. It was my home, and I never wanted to leave it.

But in this moment, I really didn't want to go see Khalid. I had barely spoken a word to the boy before. Gorgeous people intimidated me, and I was especially intimidated by men, probably because the only men on the island were the guards. There were twenty of them. Some of them were handsome as well, but not like Khalid . . .

I took a deep breath and headed toward the main courtyard. I hadn't been able to tell where he was stationed from the scrying stone, but I figured this was as good a place as any to start searching.

I found him quicker than I expected or preferred.

My heart jumped into my throat.

My palms began to sweat at seeing him. I might as well have been a lathered horse as I stared at him. He wore a thick brown leather tunic with cotton leggings underneath in the Roman style. His dark complexion stood out amongst the typical pale English skin, and his full lips and deep brown eyes intensified his unique beauty. His family had been living in England for over a hundred years, though I wasn't sure where exactly. But the handful of times I had heard him speak, his accent was Northern, like mine.

When I approached him, he bowed slightly in respect. "May I help you with something?" His voice was low-pitched and quiet toned, which instantly made my toes tingle.

I froze as his eyes stayed steady on my own. I could gaze into them for hours.

"Priestess Anna?" he prodded gently.

"I'm not a priestess yet. I'm still training," I clarified for some mortifying reason. What was wrong with me? Now he'd think I was as unkind as the girls thought I was. Before he could respond to my rudeness, I blurted, "The other priestesses-in-training are going to tell you I am in love with you and that I harbor an infatuation with you. I simply wanted you to know that they are doing this to be cruel to me. The truth is, I like you very much, and you are very handsome. Thank you." I curtsied and ran as fast as my legs would carry me.

I couldn't believe those words had spilled out of my mouth. I had promised myself that I wouldn't tell him I liked him. The only thing worse would have been having an audience. They never would have let me live it down.

Stopping under an outcropping of trees, I fell to my knees, unable to hold back the tears anymore. I had no friends, and I'd made a complete fool of myself in front of the only boy I'd ever admired.

Tucking my knees up to my chest, I lowered my head and cried into my dress. The release of all my pent-up energy turned into a good, relieving sob.

It was all my fault, really. If I hadn't been thinking of Khalid while holding the scrying stone, I never would have conjured his image. I needed to practice more, or I could summon something even more embarrassing, if that were possible.

I wiped the tears from my eyes, readying myself for the inevitable. Since I'd left class early, Bronwyn would undoubtedly be promised the stone for the week to practice, but she'd admitted to me she already knew how to use the stone. I needed it more. But after my humiliation in class, there was no way Bronwyn would give it to me willingly.

Taking a deep breath, I mentally prepared myself for my mission.

I was going to steal the scrying stone.

Chapter 2
BRONWYN

Sometimes I could be a real dolt. I used to believe it was because I was not yet an adult that I was this way, but the longer I thought about it, the more I realized I did stupid, sometimes disastrous things because I didn't *think*.

It was going well for once between Anna and me. Then I looked around at Joanna and the others and suddenly stopped thinking and fell back on what I'd been doing to fit in here: joining in. I didn't mean to hurt Anna's feelings. I never did . . . well, mostly never. Sometimes she got on my nerves so much that I wanted to turn her into something that couldn't speak, like a book. Then I could just go to her when I needed information instead of having information shoved at me at all times whether I asked for it or not.

I had a temper. High Priestess Elaine called me "impulsive" and said many times that I had to learn control. All my life people had sneered at me because I was a peasant. It wasn't like people walked around saying, "You! Peasant!" It was obvious enough without words. And in regards to Anna, I could read her judgement clearly on her face and hear it in her voice every time she spouted information at me.

After Anna left the classroom, I could focus on my stupidity because there was no one else around for Joanna or her friends to pick on.

Why hadn't I said something? Why hadn't I stuck up for Anna like I should have?

Because when it came to Anna, sometimes I wished someone would knock her down a peg or two. She knew everything and made sure everyone was aware of the fact, especially me. It was like she had to remind me about where I came from. The only reason I had learned to read and write was because my father stole books, one at a time, from his master, and my brothers and I would copy them during the night so that Father could return them the next day. Being the youngest, I was lucky to have the more difficult books my older brothers had copied waiting for me when I was ready for them.

Still, when High Priestess Elaine came to my family's home to bring me to Avalon, I understood quickly that I was not nearly as educated as the priestesses-in-training who had been on Avalon since the age of seven. Anna, with her incredible ability to absorb information as easily as breathing, was a constant reminder of what I *didn't* know. Add on her gift of bragging about it, and within a few months of living in Avalon, I understood that even trying to have a conversation with Anna meant being shot down for—what else?—being stupid.

At least I was over being afraid that people in Avalon would be scared of me. By the time I was nine or ten, people in my village started noticing that strange things happened when I was around.

13

First, a bowl or cup would be moved or broken, then a herd of goats would be in someone's home. I was identified as the strange one by the time I was twelve, and for the next two years, people stayed far away from me, whispering about me when they thought I was too far to hear, putting up charms and talismans over their doors.

I was never attacked. They were likely afraid I'd hurt them if they did, and it didn't help that I had grown as tall as my eldest brother, which was rare for a girl. But they never knew—never let me explain—that I couldn't help it most of the time. My family tried not to be afraid of me, but they didn't understand what was happening to me any more than I did. The more I was shunned, the sadder I grew, and the more damaging my magic became. Honestly, I was surprised I'd never destroyed the village. I was a disaster waiting to happen. High Priestess Elaine had saved my village by taking me away.

At the end of class, I wrapped the scrying stone carefully in cloth and double-checked that the straps on my sack were not fraying before I put the stone inside. I would not be responsible for breaking one. They were forged by specialized stonemasons over a period of years. To break one was as horrible as killing someone. Not that it would break easily, since it was a thick, heavy stone, but none of us wanted to risk it.

Joanna caught up to me as I walked out of the classroom. "It must be torture."

"What must be torture?" I asked.

"You keep getting paired with Anna. Why do you think Priestess Elaine does that anyway?"

I shrugged.

"She's so privileged."

What was Joanna doing, trying to provoke me? It had been this way for a long time. Whenever something happened between Anna and me in front of other priestesses-in-training, Joanna or Chelsea or another of that group would try to show that they were on my side. It was like they were proving some kind of loyalty. I'd never established a me-versus-Anna war, and I didn't think she had either.

I certainly didn't want a following. I didn't deserve one for any reason. I understood soon into moving to Avalon, that they sensed, and often saw, my power, and they wanted some of it in any way they could. Being my friend or my follower or whatever was their ticket to . . . what? I had no idea.

"She *is* privileged," I said. "You all are, aren't you?"

"What do you mean?" Joanna asked innocently.

"You all came here years ago, and since then, you have all had everything you've ever needed without effort. So you all are as privileged as Anna, right?"

Joanna paused for a moment. "Her family was already wealthy. She's never had to work a day in her life."

I nodded, but I knew Joanna hadn't either.

Joanna walked with me down the wide corridor, which was covered with elaborate tapestries. "I'm just saying that she thinks she's better than you. Than all of us."

Nice save, I thought. Joanna would make a fine political advisor to a king or queen someday. Still, as much as I disliked the conversation, I didn't want to make another enemy. "Yeah."

"Maybe we can be partners next time. We could ask," Joanna suggested.

"I think High Priestess Elaine is trying to teach me something by constantly pairing me with Anna," I said.

"How to deal with snobby know-it-alls?" She snorted.

More like how to take control of my powers before I kill someone. Instead, I said, "Something like that." I hefted my sack over my shoulder. "I've got to go practice. See you later." I made sure to smile at Joanna before turning to leave.

Wanting to be away from everyone in case I got carried away, I took my scrying stone into the forest beyond Avalon's fortress to a small still lake. Before I even removed the stone from my sack, I decided to work on controlling my power, something I was determined to do sooner rather than later.

There had already been a few times when my anger toward Anna had caused me to toss things or trip people or turn their skin pink or knock Anna off her stool. When I first understood that Anna hated me, I spent much of my time apologizing to her for the accidents, but she never believed me, so I stopped trying. In a way, Anna was my motivation for getting my powers under control. I really didn't want to hurt her, as much as I didn't like her. High Priestess Elaine had said from the start that I would never become a full priestess until I gained control, no matter what the situation. And because of Anna, I realized how out of control I was.

I stopped between the lake and the tree line on the dirt bank and put my things a few paces away. I found a small stick and placed it on the ground, then stared at it and concentrated on setting it on fire.

Nothing happened. I tried to visualize the stick on fire, but my imagination was not so much visual as it was emotional. I could *feel* a situation more than see it in my mind, so I tried to *feel* heat from the stick.

I opened my eyes, and the stick began to smoke. Keeping my eyes open, I continued to feel the stick burning beneath my outstretched hands.

A flame roared into existence. The stick was burning!

I jumped up and down a few times in excitement.

And then I stopped.

The roar from that little fire was awfully loud.

And it made crackling, popping sounds too.

And it was coming from behind me.

I turned to find the five trees nearest me at the tree line ablaze. For some reason, I stomped on the stick to put it out before searching for something to stop the quickly spreading fire.

The lake! I focused, trying to imagine buckets of water rising from the lake, the fire sizzling out, and steam rising into the sky. My eyes were open, so I knew right away that it wasn't working.

I closed my eyes, hoping that might help, and concentrated on the water even harder, but the crackling of the fire growing louder as it jumped to the surrounding trees was extremely distracting.

This was it.

I was going to burn down the entire island of Avalon.

Come on, water, move!

Another roar.

I opened my eyes.

The whole lake shot up and blasted the fire and the trees, flooding the floor of the forest beyond where my eyes could reach.

It put the fire out, for sure, but it also stripped limbs bare and dumped countless flopping fish all around. The water had traveled so far away, all that was left was mud, lots and lots of mud, probably all the way up the fortress.

"No!" I cried. All those poor fish! I scrambled around, scooping up as many fish as I could to toss them back into what was left of the lake, but it was gone. The entire lake was gone. There I was, standing where the lake should have been, but all that remained was a large empty basin of mud and dying fish. "Please! Someone help me!"

Thunder boomed over me. Dark clouds grew and billowed across the sky. As if someone had dumped a bucket over me, rain poured down so hard I could barely stand. I dropped the fish and ran for my sack at the tree line.

Sheets of rain tumbled deafeningly over the empty crater. As quickly as it had started, the rain stopped. The clouds slowly drifted apart, and the sun revealed a full lake again.

"Staring at them will do the fish no good," said a familiar woman's voice.

High Priestess Elaine stood behind me with her arms crossed casually across her chest. Although her hair was pure white and her eyes were deep with knowledge, there was hardly a wrinkle on her pale face.

"I . . ." That was all I could get out.

"The fish, Bronwyn."

I dropped the sack and started running. I briefly thought that I wouldn't possibly be able to save them all. Fish couldn't live more than a few minutes out of water.

By the time the last barely living fish was put back, the sun was setting. I collapsed next to my sack. I was wet and muddy and stunk of fish. It occurred to me that High Priestess Elaine must have been keeping the fish alive magically.

High Priestess Elaine watched the sky darken over the lake. The trees were still bare, but they would thrive again on their own. Trees were a lot stronger than fish. "Thank you, High Priestess Elaine."

"We all need help now and then," she said.

"Did you actually hear me calling for help?"

She nodded. "How could I not?"

"Were you nearby?"

"I was having tea with Florette in the fortress courtyard," she said.

I thought for a moment about that. If she had heard me, I must have shouted with my mind as well as my mouth. Was I telepathic too? "How?"

"I have heard you calling out for years, Bronwyn, even when I didn't know it was you. That was how I found you in your village."

"Really?"

She tilted her head toward the poor trees in response.

"I should stop trying before I do something *enormously* bad," I said. "I'm sorry about all of this."

"Bronwyn, you must continue practicing. How else will you ever gain control? If you stop training, you will no doubt lose control at some point and, like you said, do something enormously bad. This, by the way, was pretty bad."

My face flushed until I saw High Priestess Elaine's full grin. She was teasing me!

I had to smile back, though my gut wrenched from guilt about all of the life I had hurt as a result of my practicing. "What if I never gain control?"

For the first time ever, High Priestess Elaine hugged me. It was a hug like my mother used to give me when I was much younger and scared. I bit my tongue to stop myself from crying. I wanted her to think that I could be strong.

"Bronwyn," she said while still holding me, "I understand the fear of never controlling raw power. It's a great responsibility on your shoulders. A magician like Anna will always have control because she is learning to bring forth magic through incantations and books. You, like I did, must learn to hold magic back. Two very different forces."

"She's got the easy road," I nearly growled.

At that, High Priestess Elaine released me and gently put her hands on my shoulders. "What is it, Bronwyn?"

She didn't have to explain what she meant. I sighed heavily. "Anna's driving me crazy!"

"Remember that we make our own emotions, Bronwyn. No one else."

"But she's constantly putting me down, making me feel like I'm nothing."

"Again, she doesn't make you feel something."

"I know . . ." I took a deep breath. The high priestess would not end the lesson until I demonstrated it. "When she talks to me, I feel like I'm nothing. Is that better?"

"Much better. Perhaps your own feelings sometimes get in the way of how you interpret what others say to you, do you think?"

"Yes. And *I* could be right too."

"You could," she agreed. "But much like what happened here, I suggest working on controlling your emotions, understanding them and how they color your world, before something enormously bad happens between you and someone else—like Anna, for example."

"I will, High Priestess Elaine. I swear." I meant it. I didn't want to hate anyone or be hated.

"Time to head back," High Priestess Elaine said, letting go of my shoulders.

Standing still, I closed my eyes, waiting for High Priestess Elaine to transport me back with her to the fortress. My legs and arms were sore from running around tossing fish back into the lake, amd I was relieved that I wouldn't have to walk all the way back.

I heard a giggle, and then it was quiet. I opened my eyes.

High Priestess Elaine had left without me!

I wasn't upset. I deserved it. I glanced one last time at the damage I'd done to the forest. There were still some slimy rocks and things strewn about from the lake, but mainly there were a lot of downed branches. What a disaster! I decided to call myself that. "Okay, Disaster. You should get back to the fortress before you destroy more things."

Reaching for my drenched knapsack, I noticed that it wasn't nearly as bulging as it should have been. I peered inside.

"The scrying stone!"

Panicked, I searched everywhere. I ransacked the inside of the bag, pushing my fist at the wet bottom seam. It was solid. Searching the forest floor, I hefted fallen branches and dug into the muddy decaying leaves. It was getting darker and darker, making it harder to spot even the wet tan cloth that had padded the stone, let alone the gray-black stone itself. On my knees, I crawled through the mud slowly and pushed the forest covering aside as I went, crying.

The more I searched, the more I cried.

Do not *call for help!* I thought.

There was no way I would want High Priestess Elaine to show up again. Not for a lost scrying stone. "Where could it be?" I kept asking. I couldn't believe what was happening. How could a heavy stone that was flat on the bottom just roll away? Could the water from the lake have somehow picked it up and carried it? Or had it gotten buried in the mud? It was definitely possible. I had no idea the amount of power I'd put behind that spell. For all I knew, the stone had been carried deep into the forest.

Evening had arrived, only a dark purple glow on the horizon. For a moment, I sat there, seriously thinking about running away from Avalon with my soaking wet self and my empty sack. But my parents had taught us to face the consequences of our actions, no matter how unfair they may have been, so I picked up my disgusting, smelly, dirty, fishy self and slogged back to the Avalon fortress in the dark.

Chapter 3
ANNA

I made it back to my room without running into anyone. I was drenched in sweat, and not from the record-breaking sprint I had just made.

All that power.

Bronwyn had emptied the entire lake with her brain like it was nothing. If I hadn't already been holding the scrying stone, I would have run right then, abandoning my plan to steal it from her. If she could do that with a lake, what could she do to me?

It scared me so greatly, I raced as far away from Bronwyn as possible. It wasn't until I was halfway home that I realized I still clutched the sacred stone.

What if she came after me?

Surely, when she noticed the missing stone, she'd know it was me who stole it.

Who else would dare do anything against her?

I took a deep breath.

High Priestesses Florette and Elaine would never let anything happen to me. To any of us. And to use that kind of power . . .

They had to know already what Bronwyn had done.

Big magic like that didn't go unnoticed. Not by Florette or Elaine.

Maybe they were kicking her out of Avalon right now.

My heart soared at the thought.

In the meantime, I decided I should try and figure out this scrying stone before I got in trouble for "borrowing" it. Besides, if they kicked Bronwyn out of Avalon, I could say she gave it to me before she left.

My room was small, a ten-foot square box. A bed stuffed with straw and feathers was pushed against the wall. The only other furniture was a single wooden chair, a plank of wood on logs to use as a desk, and a three-foot-tall bookcase that held the twenty-two books my parents had sent with me from home. They wanted to make sure I had my own set of tomes, knowing how much comfort books gave me.

I sat on my chair and placed the scrying stone on my desk.

I couldn't believe I was taking advice from Bronwyn, but she had been right: whatever I concentrated on appeared in the stone. Unfortunately for me, it had been Khalid.

Just thinking about what I had said to him made my palms sweat with embarrassment. I'd admitted that I liked him! What was wrong with me? And the worst part was I hadn't stayed around long enough to see his response. Was he mad? Was he disgusted? Probably both. I could never set eyes on him again. I'd have to avoid him completely.

And as before, thinking of Khalid made him appear in the stone.

24

My heart skipped a beat when my eyes locked on his beautiful face, lit in orangish red from the setting sun.

He was so perfect my fingers and toes tingled at the sight of him.

Since I had vowed to never lay eyes on him again in person, maybe I could use the scrying stone to see him.

I groaned.

Was I terrible person? I stared at Khalid's flawless features. He probably thought I was some kind of monster the way I had behaved.

Viewing the stone more carefully, I lost the ability to breathe.

Joanna and her cronies.

They approached Khalid near the main square. I still held my breath as Joanna arrived at Khalid's side. I let it out in a big gust, terrified of what was going to happen next.

Then the stone emitted sound.

Sound!

I was about to hear the whole horrifying exchange!

My stomach twisted in anticipation.

Khalid greeted each girl. "Priestesses Joanna, Tara, and Beth. What can I do for you?"

His voice was soft yet commanding at the same time. Goose bumps flared up on my arms at hearing him. I was seriously a lost cause when it came to that boy.

My heart pounded in my chest as my fantasies ended in front of my face. Why did Joanna have to be so hateful and mean? Couldn't she leave me alone? And why did she have to bring Khalid into the mix? It was horrid and cruel, and even if I was a know-it-all, I didn't deserve this kind of humiliation.

Joanna smiled at Khalid in a flirty way.

It was then that I knew: she liked him too.

And from the way the other two cronies giggled behind her, so did they.

My heart sank further.

Did everyone on this island have a crush on Khalid?

While not surprising, it was painful. Why would he ever pay an annoying windbag like me any mind when he could have the stunning Priestess Joanna? She may have been a horrible person, but she was gorgeous.

And Khalid would've had to be blind not to notice.

Joanna batted her eyes and pouted her lips.

Typical.

Then she said, "You'll never guess who likes you."

Khalid didn't seem amused, which most likely meant he despised me. He didn't have to guess who liked him; he *knew* thanks to my big fat mouth.

But to my surprise, he replied, "You?"

It flustered Joanna so much that she began to stammer. "N-no, I mean . . . I think you're great, b-but . . ." She took a second to regain her composure, then plowed forward with her gossip. "No, not me. Anna." She laughed.

It was a nasty laugh. Her deliberate plan to embarrass me in front of the boy I liked was completely working.

I felt like crawling under the blankets on my bed and never coming out again, but I was consumed by the stone. I had to see what horrific reaction Khalid would have to Joanna's accusations, to the truth.

"Priestess Anna?" Khalid asked, though he knew the answer.

If the grimace on Joanna's face was any indication, she didn't like the way the conversation was going. She'd probably expected some kind of repulsion or laugh from Khalid.

My shoulders relaxed at his response. He wasn't going to play that game, at least not with Joanna. Whether he was disgusted with my confession or not, he was being a gentleman about the situation. It made me like him even more.

Joanna nodded. "Priestess-in-training, but yes, Anna. Isn't that preposterous?"

My skin burned. I was angry and disgraced all at once. I was surprised I wasn't spontaneously combusting from the varying degrees of fire burning inside me.

Khalid answered, "Preposterous? Yes. I cannot imagine a beautiful girl like Priestess Anna giving a lowly guard like me the time of day. She is far too good for me. If you'll excuse me, I have to concentrate on my duty. I must keep all of you priestesses safe."

I nearly fainted.

With that, he walked away.

I was in such shock I didn't know what to do.

He called me beautiful!

He said *I* was too good for *him*!

I wanted to run out of my room and find him and . . .

What?

I wouldn't know what to say or do. I wasn't even sure I'd be able to speak properly.

Then a horrible thought hit me.

He'd probably said all those things to protect my honor, not because he liked me. Khalid was a decent enough human being to defend me from the likes of Joanna because he felt it was the right thing to do, not because he was telling the truth.

I wished I knew for sure.

If anything, doing what he did showed me more of his

character. I already knew he was a good person because of how he treated the priestesses on the island. He was quiet and kind, always helping those in need. Saying what he'd said to Joanna was simply another compassionate gesture on his part.

At least I could see him again.

After his response, I knew he wasn't angry or repulsed. Maybe we could be friends if I could figure out how to function like a normal human being around him. Not likely, but I hoped so.

My mind couldn't help but go into fantasy mode at the thought of being with Khalid. We could be like King Arthur and Queen Guinevere, living in the Avalon fortress like our own Camelot. It was such a strong dream that it took me a few moments before I noticed the scrying stone had shifted to someone new.

Someone I had never seen before.

His hair was black as night, and his eyes were almost as dark in contrast to his alabaster skin. There was something sinister about the expression on his face, from the unbridled fury in his eyes to the way his lips tugged up in a slight sneer.

He stood in an ornate room, all the furnishings expensive and luxurious, with velvet tapestries and a gilded four-poster bed behind him. A floor-length mirror was propped against the wall, and he stared at himself as if weighing his intentions.

There was nothing likeable about him, nothing at all.

Anger radiated off his body like visible waves.

He terrified me.

As soon as the thought left my mind, his eyes snapped up in the mirror and met mine.

He saw me!

Through the scrying stone!

I hadn't even known that was possible.

I shoved the stone away, and the image disappeared.

I jumped when a familiar voice screamed from my doorway. "I should have known you would take it, you stealing thief!" Bronwyn bellowed.

Bronwyn stood in my room, now clean and dry from her earlier ordeal with the lake.

"A stealing thief is redundant. That's what a thief does: she steals. You don't have to say both," I said. My heart raced at being caught, and in my terror, I reverted back to my know-it-all default.

Bad move.

Bronwyn's eyes began to glow.

Glow!

She was going to destroy me.

I panicked. "Don't kill me like those fish!" I pictured all the fish flopping on the ground after she had demolished the lake.

This caused her eyes to return to their normal brown color. Her face softened a bit. "You saw that?"

I figured my best option was to escape by any means necessary, but she brought out the worst in me. "Yes, I saw that, and when High Priestesses Elaine and Florette find out, they'll kick you out of Avalon, so leave before I tell them!"

Bronwyn's rage returned. "High Priestess Elaine already knows, and she put the lake back where it belongs!"

"What?" My blood boiled. "What a shock! Bronwyn does something completely against the rules and extremely dangerous and is forgiven without punishment!"

Bronwyn reared her head back. "I don't get special treatment," she said defensively.

"Oh really? You think any other girl would have been allowed to stay in Avalon after emptying a *lake*? You're delusional! You've been treated with kid gloves ever since you arrived! Probably because they're scared of you! I know I am!" A weight lifted from my chest at confessing all my pent-up emotion. It was terribly unfair how Bronwyn always managed to escape punishment, and I was finally able to voice my fury.

Bronwyn's face was frozen in surprise. "You're scared of me?"

I could have calmed down and possibly had a real conversation with Bronwyn, but I was too far in the red of my hatred of the last two years of torture. Of the girl who had been the reason for all of it. Of my isolation. Of my loss of friends. Of my utter loneliness. It was all *her*. Her! "Yes! I'm terrified of you and your power! If you can set fire to a forest and put it out with a *lake*, what else can you do? And I'm enemy number one in your world, so of course I'm scared. Look how you stormed in here screaming at me, calling me names! Incorrect names," I added in my rage.

"See!" Bronwyn was angry again. "You can't have one single conversation with me without correcting me, judging me, or treating me like I'm an uneducated idiot! I wasn't raised here like you. I didn't have access to teachers and the books in the Avalon library. Everything I learned was hard-won and difficult. I'm not stupid, but you've made me feel that way every day I've been here!"

"Don't you dare put this back on me! You're the one who has friends. You're the one who ridicules me in public. You're the one who has made my life intolerable. People actually liked me before you came. Now everyone hates me, and I'm completely alone!" My voice caught as tears filled my eyes. The pain of admitting that out loud twisted my stomach.

Bronwyn froze. Her mouth opened and closed several times, but no words came out. Had she finally heard me? Would she finally take responsibility for the anguish she'd caused me since she came to

Avalon?

Nope.

"You can't blame me for your annoying personality," Bronwyn snapped. "You constantly put people down and lord your intelligence over everyone. I didn't make your friends abandon you. I would never do that! My village was terrified of me, so I know what it's like to be alone. I would never do that to another human being. Not even you!"

"Well, you did. And by the way, nothing has changed. We're all still scared of you!" I was so mad that she hadn't heard a word I'd said. She still acted as if her behavior was acceptable.

"You don't know anything!" Bronwyn yelled. "I have complete control over my powers!"

"Yeah, well, those fish say otherwise!" I crossed my arms angrily.

A white glowing ball of energy escaped from Bronwyn's hands and hit me square in the chest. It knocked the wind out of me, and I gasped for air.

Bronwyn ran to my side. "I'm so sorry! I didn't mean—"

"Liar! You absolutely meant to hit me with that energy ball!" I incanted the only spell I knew off the top of my head: levitation. I sent the scrying stone flying off my desk and straight into Bronwyn's chest.

She flew back a few feet from the impact and fell to the floor on her rump.

I'd never know what magic she might have thrown at me after that because High Priestess Elaine suddenly appeared in the doorway.

"That will be enough! You girls are coming with me!"

I cringed.

Uh-oh.

Chapter 4
BRONWYN

I wasn't sure if my stomach hurt so badly because of the scrying stone Anna had hurled at me or because I was certain I was about to be kicked out of Avalon. My only consolation was that if I was going, so was Anna, and she had no survival skills. As we followed High Priestess Elaine through the halls, I pictured Anna alone in the forest and wandering the roads of England, not knowing the difference between a sweet little squirrel and an angry wild boar and being gutted by the boar. I thought of a lot of gruesome ways Anna would perish outside of Avalon in that short period of time.

Not only was Anna a know-it-all prude, but she was also a thief. I'd been given the scrying stone for practice. But no, she had to have it. She couldn't wait. She actually tracked me deep into the forest to take it. What nerve!

She obviously felt like she needed the practice since she'd embarrassed herself in front of the whole class. She had to have some seriously deep feelings for Khalid to have unintentionally called him up on the scrying stone. Khalid was so out of her league. Anna was pretty, but Khalid was like a god. Maybe that was why she'd decided to steal the stone from me. She wanted to stare at him without him knowing. Creepy. And it was because of *her* that I was on my way to being expelled!

I kept my head down, not caring to speak with anyone as we walked through the halls. I stared at the back of High Priestess Elaine's boots and the hem of her robe. A part of me wanted to break into a run and flee Avalon on my own. Every time I got into an argument with Anna, a voice in my head reminded me that this was not proper behavior for a priestess-in-training, that someday it would all come back to bite me and that someone would have enough of me. I tried so hard in the beginning to hold my temper. But Anna gnawed at my self-control like water constantly dripping on stone. And here I was, following the woman I idolized to pay for all of that incorrect behavior. My throat thickened with shame.

It took all my concentration to keep my hands from trembling with rage. I never once looked at Anna, even when we arrived at High Priestess Florette's chambers and High Priestess Elaine opened the large oak double doors. I stepped through first and stood in front of the leaders of Avalon with my head down, staring at the dark woven rug beneath my boots, Anna's boots right next to me. I thought about how shiny they were.

"You are correct to feel ashamed of your behavior," High Priestess Florette said in an even tone. I didn't make eye contact, too afraid of how she'd look at me. "Such disrespect is unacceptable for a priestess of Avalon." She must have been talking to me. "One would have hoped that the years you have been with us taught you differently. I expected more from you." I changed my mind. She had to be talking about Anna. Anna always behaved. I glimpsed over at Anna's reaction. Her head was down too. A giant tear fell from her eye and tapped her boot. My heart squeezed in a moment of sympathy. I was used to being scolded, but she wasn't. "A priestess of Avalon never turns away from what frightens her!" High Priestess Florette's voice was so strong that the walls could have been vibrating.

I looked at her, wanting very much to avert my gaze again. High Priestess Florette sat behind a simple wooden desk, her hands clasped together on its surface. A tapestry of the Avalon fortress framed the room, with Florette dead center. Her lips pressed together as she eyed each of us in turn.

Gulp.

"Anna and Bronwyn, you will learn to appreciate the differences between you or we are all doomed," High Priestess Florette said with finality.

Doomed? Why did it suddenly feel like the entire fate of Avalon rested on my shoulders, *our* shoulders? Which was what I supposed she meant, but why us? I wanted to ask the question, but there was no way I was going to open my mouth. Something stupid would have come out of it.

"Doomed? That was quite dramatic of you, Florette," High Priestess Elaine said in a surprisingly light tone.

"Perhaps," High Priestess Florette said, "but it isn't necessarily incorrect."

"True."

Were they having a casual conversation in front of us? What happened to the anger and disappointment?

I took a risk and slowly raised my hand like I was in class.

"Yes?" High Priestess Florette said in a less friendly tone than she'd used with High Priestess Elaine.

"How can we be responsible for causing . . . doom?"

Anna nodded slightly. She was obviously thinking the same thing.

"You, Bronwyn, and you, Anna, are to be the next high priestesses of Avalon."

Excuse me?

What?

High Priestess Florette continued. "Elaine has placed the two of you together over and over again with the hope that you would have learned to get along by now. Clearly, our hopes have been dashed."

Elaine sighed deeply. "You are both intelligent, talented young women. If you had bothered to observe one another for signs of friendship rather than for something to criticize, you might have found some peace with each other. Now, we see no other choice."

I was still stuck on us being the next high priestesses of Avalon. Looking at Anna, I noticed her wide eyes and the slight shake of her hands. She was scared.

"Have either of you anything to say?" High Priestess Florette asked.

I didn't.

And apparently, neither did Anna.

"Keeping the two of you here within the safety of Avalon is doing no good . . . for any of us," High Priestess Elaine said.

"You must learn to work together as if your lives depended upon it," said High Priestess Florette.

"Because they will," said High Priestess Elaine.

My mouth fell open. Doom? Our lives depended upon something? Were they going to throw us into a pit full of wolves?

"Anna and Bronwyn, you are both hereby banished from

35

Avalon. You will not be permitted to return until you have mastered your gifts and become the true leaders of our order." High Priestess Florette leaned back in her chair and folded her hands in her lap. She was not smiling, nor was she frowning. She wasn't angry. She was . . . stating the facts.

We were banished.

Elaine took two steps forward and grabbed both my hand and Anna's.

This was getting serious.

Elaine closed her eyes in concentration, and her hands began to glow a brilliant white, like fire, though I felt no burning on my skin.

In a quick burst, the light traveled through her hands and into both our bodies. My eyes flew to Anna's, and her face froze in horror as we both glowed brightly.

Elaine, just as suddenly, released her grip, and the light dissipated entirely.

My body shuddered for a moment afterward, and Anna lurched forward a step.

What had happened?

"From this moment forward," High Priestess Florette said, "you are bound to each other. One of you cannot travel without the other. You will share your fates."

Share? That didn't sound good.

I took a step away from Anna and glanced at the high priestesses. They watched me, but as they said nothing, I took another step. Anna's eyes were trained on me now. She took a step in the other direction. After another couple of steps, I jumped.

Anna jerked in my direction, almost tripping to the floor. "Hey!"

"That's enough, Bronwyn," High Priestess Florette said.

It was true.

We were magically bound to each other.

Physically.

What kind of nightmare was this?

We could possibly have some privacy around a tree, but that was about it.

"Where will we go?" Anna asked, terror causing her voice to shake. "What do we do?"

"You will travel to Camelot, where you will continue to train under the Wizard Merlin," High Priestess Elaine said. "You will represent Avalon with all of the grace and power expected of priestesses in the court of King Arthur."

Anna and I turned to each other. A hint of wonder lit up her face, and I was sure mine reflected the same awe. Arthur had been king for many years. He had unified much of England in the face of continued invasion. The Wizard Merlin was, well, legendary. Some people said that he lived backward in time. Some said he knew the words that would open an underworld where he could renew his powers. What everyone in Avalon knew was that he used magic to ensure that Arthur would become king. Why? That was forever a mystery.

And he would teach *us*!

Merlin didn't use magic like the priestesses of Avalon. He didn't follow rules. That would most definitely frustrate Anna. But not me!

"But," Anna said, "the Wizard Merlin is . . ." She paused and dropped her head down. "He uses raw magic."

Exactly! I thought. Of course she would be frightened. The Wizard Merlin was known for what happened when he lost his temper, which wasn't often. I imagined him looming over Anna, coming down on her like thunderbolts.

"As do you, Anna," High Priestess Florette said kindly. "We all use raw magic. Priestesses like you require incantations to tame it."

Anna exhaled as she lifted her head. High Priestess Florette stood and walked around the table. She stood face-to-face with Anna and smiled. "I do too."

High Priestess Elaine took a large oval copper mirror out from a cabinet on the wall and stood it up against a leg of the desk. High Priestess Elaine passed her hand over the surface of the mirror. Like me, she could use her innate power without having to perform incantations.

The surface of the mirror glowed and then dimmed to reveal the ageless yet ancient face of the Wizard Merlin. His silver hair was cut short in the Roman style. Behind him was a gray stone wall and a shelf with an assortment of ancient tomes, bottles of powders and liquids, and a couple items I couldn't recognize.

"Ladies, your timing is impeccable," Merlin said. "I was sitting down to tea." His gaze moved to Anna and me. "These are the priestesses-in-training?"

High Priestess Elaine nodded. "Anna and Bronwyn," she said, indicating each of us as she said our names. "We have decided to send them a little early, if that is acceptable."

"Quite," Merlin said. Something caught Merlin's eyes beyond his mirror, and he motioned with his hand. There was a rustling out of view that caused Merlin to frown. "Just—" he said and motioned again.

A young man stepped into view. I didn't see his face at first because he was busy untangling something from his hair that was tied behind his head. He finally lifted his head. I felt like someone had lit a fire near my face. I inhaled loudly. Anna raised an eyebrow at me.

He was simply adorable!

He grinned at us.

"Houdain will meet the priestesses outside of Camelot and bring them to court," Merlin said.

High Priestess Florette said, "Excellent. Avalon is taking a more active role in the affairs of England." She focused on us. "Anna and Bronwyn, rather than remaining in the shadows as high priestesses in the past have, you will be known by all at the end of your training."

Merlin and the high priestesses stared at us. Houdain, that beautiful boy, continued to grin.

Anna and I shared shocked glances. This was really going to happen!

"Gather your things," High Priestess Florette said. "You leave at once."

There was nothing else to say. With a wave of Elaine's hand, we left High Priestess Florette's room, Merlin still in the mirror, no doubt to decide the details of our training.

Anna and I walked together, lips sealed as we made our way back to our rooms. No longer furious at Anna, I came to terms with the fact that it was as much my fault as it was hers. I was more horrified that I had to leave Avalon. It was nighttime now, so the halls were practically empty, most of the girls in their rooms for the night.

We were stuck together—literally. Curious, I slowed down and left enough room for a passing priestess to walk between us, which she did easily.

"Don't even try," Anna said. "Only the person who cast the

binding spell can break it."

"I wasn't trying to break it. I was trying to see what would happen if someone got between us," I said.

"It only affects you and me."

"I noticed."

"Where have you been?" Joanna came up next to me, dressed in her sleeping gown. "And why are you with *her*?"

I stopped walking to talk to Joanna, but I was yanked forward by Anna, who had obviously not stopped. "Can't talk!" I called back at her as I regained my balance.

Joanna caught up with me, but with enough distance so that Anna couldn't hear us. "What's going on? Are you mad at me or something?"

"No, not at all. I'm just . . . distracted." I wasn't ready to tell anyone about our banishment yet. I was too embarrassed.

"Did Anna say something to you? You know she lies about things." Joanna spoke quickly.

If Joanna had some kind of information about Anna I could use against her someday, I needed to have it. "She's full of lies," I said. "What do you know?"

"Well," she said, settling in beside me. She took a breath, but before she could speak, I was yanked forward again.

Anna glanced over her shoulder at me, eyebrows furrowed. Definitely angry.

Joanna caught up again. "What are you doing?"

"You can't tell?" I asked sarcastically. "I've been bound to Anna permanently." I didn't believe it was permanent, but I felt like being dramatic. And in that moment, I decided to tell Joanna what had happened, or at least *my* version of what had happened. A perfect opportunity to leave behind an impression. Anna kept walking briskly, so I allowed myself to trip a little, appearing more helpless than I was. "She got us kicked out of Avalon," I said, and Joanna's jaw dropped.

"What did she do?" she asked, almost drooling for gossip.

"She stole from me and then provoked me into a fight. It was the last straw for the high priestesses, so they gave us the boot. Banished."

"For good?" she asked, hooked.

"Gotta go!" I said, jogging to catch up to Anna.

Joanna stopped, gawking after me. She turned around and raced off, no doubt to tell everyone, even if they were asleep.

What I'd told Joanna would spread like wildfire. Whatever happened to us on the outside, at least I knew that here in Avalon, the only place I truly loved, Anna would no longer be remembered as the good girl.

Chapter 5
ANNA

Really? As if everyone didn't hate me enough, now Bronwyn had officially made it impossible for me to have friends on this island. Ever. I'd forever be branded as the girl who made the precious Bronwyn go away. And it was *her* fault we were in this mess, not mine! She'd attacked me with some kind of light ball! I'd been defending myself when I used the scrying stone as a cannonball to Bronwyn's gut.

I smiled inwardly. I'd always cherish that moment when the stone knocked the wind out of her. That tiny *umph* of shock that had come out of her lungs would be my own piece of paradise for years to come.

And considering I fully expected my life to be pure torture from now on being bound to Bronwyn, I needed all the paradise I could get.

Bound.

How had this happened?

It was easier to focus on my annoyances with Bronwyn than what I really should've been focused on: the fact that High Priestesses Florette and Elaine had just told us we were to be the next high priestesses of Avalon.

I barely thought I'd graduate, let alone lead the entire island of priestesses. An island that would despise me. Priestess Florette didn't understand how much the other girls hated me. They didn't listen now, so why would they listen later on? Bronwyn would be worshipped and revered even more so than she was today. I'd be the evil crone who'd somehow spelled her way into power, who'd magically tied herself to the precious princess in order to steal the position as high priestess, who'd secretly plotted against the illustrious Bronwyn for her own selfish gains.

And Bronwyn would sit back and enjoy all of it. She reveled in my despair; I could see it in her eyes.

She'd talked to Joanna like I couldn't hear her, putting thoughts into Joanna's puny little brain. The island would be buzzing with how I was responsible for banishing Bronwyn. It wasn't fair. I wouldn't be able to defend myself. No one believed a word I said anyway. No one cared.

I was truly alone.

Tears threatened to overcome me yet again.

Banished from my home. The girls may not have liked me, but the island did. I could feel it with every step I took on Avalon. It was a living entity, and it loved me. It loved all of us. And now I was being forced to leave it.

With Bronwyn.

Camelot was at least a small perk. Meeting Merlin would be both terrifying and exciting. Maybe, for once, someone would see through Bronwyn's nice-girl act.

43

Bronwyn caught up to me as I stormed toward our dorms. "Our rooms are too far apart to pack separately, so we'll go to my room first since it's closest."

"What a surprise, always thinking of yourself." How selfish could one person be? She hadn't even asked or offered to go to my room first.

Bronwyn rolled her eyes. "It's closer. I'm trying to save us some time."

"Are you in such a rush to leave? I want to enjoy the last moments I have here." I *did* want to leave as soon as possible for simple fear of being mobbed by Joanna and her army of crones, despite what time of night it was. It wouldn't have surprised me if they were planning some kind of revolt that would involve torturing me somehow.

"Are you going to argue with me every minute of every day for the rest of our lives?" Bronwyn stared at me as if I were an annoying child she was forced to take care of.

If I said anything to contradict her, it would only prove her point, so I simply sighed. "Fine. We'll go to your room first. Lead the way."

Bronwyn almost seemed disappointed that I hadn't fallen into her trap, always desperate to be right and smarter than everyone else. It gave me a smug sense of satisfaction that I was too clever for her scheming. It may have been a small victory, but it was still a victory.

I decided to keep my mouth shut from then on. I'd let her be the bad guy. If I stayed quiet, then no one could misconstrue what I said. It would be difficult if she started lying about me like she always did, but I was determined to be the bigger person. Saying mean things about me in front of others while I was standing next to her would only show people how vicious she really was.

It didn't take long to reach Bronwyn's room, and the quiet was nice. Maybe the silent treatment would be a great solution to our *bonding* issue. As long as the girl kept her mouth shut too, life wouldn't be so terrible.

I stood in the doorway while Bronwyn shoved some clothes and personal items into a leather rucksack. I was taken aback by her room. I'd never seen it before since I had no reason to visit my torturer. But I was surprised that it was so empty. I had expected Bronwyn to have every accolade she'd ever earned (and there were a lot of them) displayed on her shelves, but there was none of that. Aside from a shelf, a desk, and a bed like mine, there were only a few books, an ink set with parchment, and not much else.

She must have picked up on my befuddlement because she said, "What did you expect to see?"

I shrugged. "Something more extravagant."

"That's more for rich girls like you," she answered snidely.

Bite my tongue. Bite my tongue. Bite my tongue.

When Bronwyn received no response from me, she finally turned away and stuffed the last of her things into her bag. Then she nodded to the hallway. "Let's go."

I took great pleasure in the fact that my nonargumentative behavior was beginning to bother her. She fidgeted with the leather strap of her bag and kept eyeing me, then turned away. It was almost as if we were in a staring contest and whoever yelled first would lose.

I took a deep, calming breath. I would win this battle. Bronwyn had no patience for strategy. She was too emotional and impulsive. I was determined to make her break. Then maybe someone would see that I wasn't the antagonist. That she usually started our screaming matches. That I was simply defending myself. I was never the instigator.

We walked across the courtyard, which was lit by torches every few feet, and made our way to my sleeping quarters. Entering only enraged me more since it was still a disaster from our altercation.

Bronwyn watched with a smirk of satisfaction as I rummaged through the debris to find what I wanted to bring with me. Not much, I decided. Clothes, a hairbrush, and my favorite spell book would do nicely. It was rather liberating not being bogged down with possessions. Having the ability to live off a barely filled rucksack was freeing somehow.

I turned to Bronwyn. "Now what? We just leave? At night?"

A flash of fear crossed her features, then she hid it with a shrug of her shoulders. "I guess."

"Do you think it's a test? Maybe as the next leaders of Avalon we should automatically know what to do?" Seeing the dread in her eyes at my questions only amplified my own terror.

"We should make our way to the shores," Bronwyn suggested.

"At the skiff where we first arrived," I added.

Bronwyn led the way, and for once we were on the same page.

"Are you nervous?" I asked.

Instead of putting up a wall of defensiveness, as I expected, Bronwyn nodded. "Yeah, a little."

Progress. Maybe me refusing to rise to her taunting would steer us to a more civilized relationship. I didn't want to put too much faith in the prospect, but if we were truly bound to each other, then it gave me a shred of hope that it might not be so bad in the future.

"You can't leave with Bronwyn. We won't let you."

I turned around to see Joanna with nearly our entire class

46

standing behind her, most of them in their dressing gowns, half asleep.

Bronwyn covered her mouth in shock.

It was as I suspected. Joanna had riled up the troops.

And here they were, about to tar and feather me for trying to take "their Bronwyn" away.

Bronwyn stepped forward. "I may have exaggerated Anna's guilt in all this—"

Joanna cut her off. "Don't worry, Bronwyn. You don't have to cover for her. We know Anna attacked you. We're on our way to the high priestesses now to protest your banishment. Anna should be punished, not you."

I rolled my eyes with Joanna's every word. It was easier to act annoyed than to show what I truly felt: anguish. Seeing almost everyone I knew in front of me, snarling at me, wanting me gone from my home . . . It was more painful than I could bear.

I didn't say a word. What could I say? They had made up their minds, and nothing I did or said would change that.

Bronwyn's reaction was the opposite of mine. She seemed . . . touched. And who wouldn't be? These girls loved her so much they were willing to fight for her to stay.

Her eyes met mine, and I saw something there I hadn't expected: guilt.

At least it was something. Bronwyn obviously hadn't realized that Joanna's hatred of me ran so deep. She barely needed a spark to ignite that particular blaze. It didn't help that Khalid had basically told her to get lost and that *I* was beautiful.

I was still reeling from that one.

Bronwyn sighed heavily. "For better or worse, Anna and I are bound to each other. We *have* to leave the island. Thank you for your loyalty and friendship though. I'll never forget it."

Joanna wasn't ready to give up. "Bronwyn, we can fix this. High Priestesses Elaine and Florette can't refuse our whole class!"

"We can, and we will!" Elaine's voice boomed from seemingly nowhere.

The older priestess suddenly appeared in the middle of the face-off.

Elaine addressed the entire group. "Despite what you girls may think, High Priestess Florette and I actually know what we're doing. Priestesses Bronwyn and Anna *will* be leaving Avalon, and the decision is final." Elaine focused her gaze on Joanna. "Do you understand, Priestess Joanna?"

I loved watching Joanna squirm. She nodded immediately, probably in fear of being kicked out herself.

Elaine wasn't finished though. "And contrary to what you may have heard"—she eyed Bronwyn with a stern expression—"*both* Priestesses Anna and Bronwyn were at fault for their actions, which is why *both* priestesses will have to suffer the consequences."

Bronwyn's cheeks reddened from embarrassment, and I would have giggled from happiness if I weren't so terrified. After angering Priestess Elaine earlier, the last thing I wanted to do was make it worse. She might've turned me into a frog or something. But it cushioned the sting of seeing all the priestesses-in-training turning on me. I hoped they'd believe Priestess Elaine. Maybe in time they could like me.

"Now go back to your rooms and get some sleep so these girls can get to the shore," Priestess Elaine ordered.

I was relieved she hadn't let Joanna and the others say their goodbyes. If she had, it would have been horribly one-sided. I would have had to stand and watch as everyone hugged Bronwyn, giving her their best wishes while throwing me dirty looks. Priestess Elaine most likely knew that and had saved me the humiliation.

Bronwyn didn't say a word to me as we walked away from the scene. We each grabbed a torch in the courtyard and made our way to the shore.

To my dread, it didn't take long. A single wooden skiff with a set of oars awaited the two of us.

Bronwyn waved her hand for me to enter the small boat. "After you."

"Not yet."

We turned around to see High Priestess Florette and . . .

Khalid.

I couldn't move or speak. What was he doing here? He had no idea I had witnessed his heroic defense of my character through the scrying stone. No, my last experience with Khalid was when I told him I liked him and ran back to my room. Very mature.

High Priestess Florette motioned Khalid toward us. "Khalid will be your personal guard at Camelot. I want to make sure you girls are safe on your journey."

Bronwyn bowed slightly. "Thank you, High Priestess Florette. Khalid will be a welcome companion." She chuckled in my direction. Bronwyn knew of my crush on Khalid and was obviously relishing every awkward moment.

I turned to thank Priestess Florette, but my ability to speak was long gone, so I nodded and smiled.

She didn't seem to mind as she bowed back to us. "Safe journey, priestesses." Then she left us.

Alone.

With Khalid.

Before I embarrassed myself further, I climbed into the skiff

49

while trying to balance my torch and sat in the center so I wouldn't capsize the boat. It would've been just my luck to fall into the lake of Avalon in front of the boy I liked.

I had been so focused on getting into the boat without mishap that I hadn't noticed Khalid's hand, which he had held out to help me in. I stammered what I thought was an apology but sounded more like a cat yacking up a fur ball.

To my horror, Bronwyn laughed. I wanted to punch her, but if I did it was a guarantee I'd fall into the water. She gladly took Khalid's hand and let him seat her on the bench next to me. She whispered in my ear, "You're a mess, and it's completely obvious. Relax, he's just a guy. Granted, a really beautiful one, but still."

I didn't respond. I physically wasn't able to. Bronwyn pointing out that I was a wreck made it so much worse. At least we were only lit by torchlight. I hoped it hid the flush in my face.

Khalid, thankfully, kept to his usual stoic nature and didn't appear bothered by my lack of social etiquette. Thank the Goddess for his Avalon guard training. Inside, he was probably thinking I was a complete idiot.

As he sat down across from us, Khalid took the oars and began to row toward the giant wall of mist that separated Avalon from the rest of England.

"Time to part the mists. You ready?" Bronwyn asked.

Worried my paralyzing shyness might prevent us from leaving the island, I took a deep breath and closed my eyes. Out of sight, out of mind. If Khalid's gorgeous face wasn't in front of me, maybe I could pretend he wasn't there.

"I'll speak the words, and you conjure the magic," I said calmly.

We each held a torch in one hand, and I was surprised to feel Bronwyn's other hand shaking as she lifted it to part the mist.

She was more nervous than I was. For me, it was about a boy; for her, it was about controlling her magic. My chest tightened in a moment of sympathy for Bronwyn. It must've been difficult for her to control all the power she had bottled inside. The kind of conjuring magic I used only worked when the words were said correctly, so if I messed up, no harm was done. But with innate magic, *lakes* were emptied!

I spoke the Latin words to perfection, if I did say so myself, and when my eyes opened, we were on the shores of England.

Crisp against my face, the wind blew hard against us, and even in the darkness of night, the clouds above were black and swollen. Rain was a certainty at this point. I hadn't been back to England since I'd left for Avalon, and a mixture of emotion roiled inside me. I came from a good family. We weren't rich, but we were privileged. I'd grown up learning all the social niceties a lady needed to know, but I'd been beyond thrilled when I was chosen by Avalon. The last thing I had wanted was to be married off to some lord and be his possession for the rest of my life.

Khalid jumped out of the skiff and pulled it onto the sand. This time he wasn't taking no for an answer. He held his hand out directly in front of me.

I tried to stop my hand from shaking as I grasped his. I nearly gasped from the tingling sensation at his touch. He placed his other hand over mine to stop it from shaking. "I'll make a fire to warm you. We need to make camp for the night."

My knees almost buckled. He mistook my shaking for coldness. Small favors.

After making sure I was securely on shore, he helped Bronwyn out of the boat as well. She shook her head with a laugh at my obvious awkwardness.

"I'm glad I can amuse you," I mumbled under my breath.

"Me too." She smiled annoyingly.

Khalid spoke before I could respond to her. "There's a clearing in the forest where we can have shelter from the rain for the night. We're only a day's walk from Camelot."

I nodded, and we followed Khalid into the giant silhouette of the forest looming in front of us, our torches casting even darker shadows.

Butterflies ran rampant in my belly from both excitement and terror.

I was excited because we were going to Camelot and terrified because I'd be seeing Khalid every day.

Okay, maybe I was more excited than terrified.

I hoped I'd be able to sleep tonight.

The clearing Khalid spoke of was smaller than I had expected, but it was enough room for three people, and the thick pine branches above us were naturally weaved together. They would keep us dry for the night. My heart raced as I wondered suddenly if Khalid would be sharing our sleeping space. He had already gathered as much dry kindling as he could find, considering it had obviously rained earlier in the day, and began to strike his flint and steel to make a fire.

Khalid grumbled, as each time he created a spark, it would instantly sizzle out. Finally, after almost an hour of trying (and us staring) he said, "The wood is too wet. I'm not sure I can make us a fire tonight."

His chin dipped down in embarrassment, and it broke my heart. I wanted to make him feel better, so I blurted, "Bronwyn, you can make a fire without an incantation. Why don't you go ahead and do that for us?"

Bronwyn's face paled. She whispered harshly, "Are you forgetting about earlier today when I almost burned Avalon down?"

I whispered back, "Just don't do that this time."

Eyeing me with shock, Bronwyn grimaced.

I didn't want her to burn our camp down, but seeing Khalid upset overruled any fears (of mine, anyway). Bronwyn would have to deal with her own issues. I honestly didn't care. I was freezing, and Khalid was upset, so that was enough for me.

Bronwyn swallowed hard, then nodded to Khalid. "Of course. That shouldn't be a problem."

I motioned to the small pile of kindling. "By all means."

Bronwyn shot me an irritated glance.

Khalid stood and bowed slightly. "Thank you, Priestess Bronwyn. I will gather branches to keep the fire going." He took a small axe from his pack and walked into the forest to start collecting pine branches.

Bronwyn whirled on me. "Thanks a lot!"

"What? I'm freezing."

"You know I emptied a lake because I set those trees on fire, yet you volunteer my services? You *want* me to fail so you'll somehow look good in front of Khalid!"

"Priestesses Florette and Elaine said we were supposed to go on this journey to learn about ourselves and our powers. So take a deep breath, concentrate, and get us warm." I toned down my attitude, but it was difficult for me since . . . well, since she drove me insane!

Khalid came back with several large pine branches balanced over his shoulder. He placed them on the ground, then left to chop down some more.

Bronwyn shook her head. "He's going to notice you staring at him all the time." Then she paused, unsure. "I think Joanna told Khalid you like him."

I eyed her carefully for any sign of a mocking nature, but I found none. Bronwyn genuinely appeared . . . responsible.

Peering over my shoulder to make sure Khalid wasn't in earshot, I said, "Well, she did, but not before I told him first. Like a fool. I ran away before I could see his reaction."

Bronwyn sighed as if exhausted. "I really am sorry about that. I should have stopped Joanna."

I didn't want to set Bronwyn off and ruin the moment since she was actually being . . . decent.

"I saw Joanna tell Khalid I liked him in the scrying stone after I ran away. He said *I* was too good for him." I shrugged, turning away in embarrassment. "He only said that to be a gentleman, but I appreciate it all the same. Someone as perfect as Khalid would never be interested in me. He's too beautiful and kind and . . . perfect. I said that already, but he really is. I'm an idiot." When my eyes met Bronwyn's again, she had a strange expression on her face. "What is it?"

My eyes squeezed shut at the sound of Khalid's voice right behind me. "I'll start chopping the wood."

Oh. My. Goddess.

I wanted to crawl under a boulder and let it flatten me.

Khalid acted as if he hadn't heard every humiliating word I had uttered. Great. Now he'd think I was an obsessed crazy person. I listened as he chopped wood for the nonexistent fire, not able to look at him.

Bronwyn's nose wrinkled in pity, and I wanted to scream. I pointed to the kindling. "Fire, please."

Bronwyn jumped at the command. I was pretty sure I'd never

seen her jump at any command of mine, so at least there was something positive out of all this.

"Right," Bronwyn said.

I kept my gaze on Bronwyn, not daring to turn around to see how Khalid would view me now. I couldn't bear it if his eyes mirrored the same pity Bronwyn had in hers. It would destroy me.

Bronwyn kneeled over the kindling and closed her eyes. After a moment or two, she opened them with a disgusted grunt. "I'm too afraid."

It took a lot for her to admit that, to me especially.

In order to escape facing Khalid, I walked over and kneeled beside her. "I know an incantation that can create a spark. It's not enough to start a fire on its own, but maybe if we work together?" I posed it as a question.

Bronwyn nodded, her expression almost humble. Almost.

"Ready?" I asked.

"Ready," she answered.

I incanted the small spell. A spark of fire appeared over the kindling. Bronwyn closed her eyes.

Whoosh!

A giant fireball blasted me away from the kindling and straight into the perfectly stacked branches Khalid had set up, destroying all his work.

Bronwyn raced over to me, a bonfire raging behind her. The heat was so intense I couldn't tell if I was on fire or if it was the heat from the newly formed flames. "Anna, are you all right? I'm so sorry, I didn't mean . . ."

I was about to yell at her with the rage coursing through my veins, knowing she had done it on purpose. If it had truly been an accident, *she* would have been blasted away as well.

But . . .

Khalid rushed to my side and held me gently in his arms, and it stopped my tirade cold. "Priestess Anna, are you injured?"

Words? What are those?

Khalid's eyes were wide and full of concern, his arms solid and strong as he held me in a sitting position. My hands began to shake. "Priestess Anna?" He turned to Bronwyn. "Take a rag from my bag. We have to see if she's burned beneath this soot."

Hands black from the blast of the fire, I grumbled.

Thanks, Bronwyn, thanks.

Bronwyn rushed to do as Khalid had instructed, which made me believe it may have actually been an accident. At least the forest wasn't on fire.

"I'm okay," I finally uttered. "I'm a little dazed. And cold." I wanted an explanation for the shaking again since it had nothing to do with temperature and everything to do with Khalid holding me.

Bronwyn hurried over with the cloth, her face racked with worry. In that instant, I knew she wasn't faking. It made me feel a little better.

My insides did flip-flops as Khalid lifted me into his arms and brought me to the roaring fire. "Is this better?" he asked, his beautiful face so close to mine. Since words still eluded me, I simply nodded.

Khalid gently wiped the soot from my face. "I don't see any burns."

"I-I'm really fine," I stammered. "I wasn't injured."

Then he smiled at me.

My whole body squeezed like I was in a vise.

"I'm glad you're okay," Khalid said quietly as he brushed my cheek with the soft cloth.

Flustered, I said, "I ruined your stack of wood."

He laughed. "Don't worry about that. With the size of this fire, that kindling will burn up fast. I'll need to put the whole stack in." Then Khalid's face went back into guard mode, and my heart dropped. "Speaking of which, I'd better get to it so you can sleep warmly tonight. There's a fresh stream a little past this clearing where you can clean up tomorrow morning. Tonight would be too cold."

"Oh, okay, thanks."

Khalid stood up and walked back, collecting the fallen firewood.

Bronwyn sat down next to me. The flames warmed my bones from the cold night. "I would have given you guys some privacy, but, you know . . . bound to you and all."

"His duty is guarding us. He was worried one of his charges had been hurt."

Bronwyn shook her head. "Maybe, but I saw the way he looked at you. And carrying you to the fire was swoon worthy. Don't you think?"

A smile spread across my face before I could stop it. "Definitely swoon worthy."

Were Bronwyn and I actually having a civil conversation? I was too afraid to say anything else for fear of setting her off.

Glancing over her shoulder, Bronwyn nodded toward Khalid as he headed over to put more wood on the fire. "We should get some sleep. We have a big day tomorrow."

In all the excitement, I had almost forgotten.

Camelot.

I took a deep breath and hoped this soot would come out of my skin and hair before we reached court.

Chapter 6
BRONWYN

I woke barely after sunrise, the trees more black than brown and green. The tree branches above us were so closely knit together that not even the slightest glow of light made it between the pine needles above me. Anna was still asleep as I stood and stretched my legs. I didn't get far though. I'd forgotten about the invisible bond between us. I debated whether or not to yank Anna awake with a small jump but thought better of it. No need to start the day antagonizing her.

There was no sign of Khalid, but I knew he was nearby. That was the strangest thing about Avalon guards. They possessed no magic, but their training involved more than being able to handle weapons and being willing to put themselves between us and danger. It was no jest when people said that Avalon guards were never seen unless they wanted to be seen. Like priestesses-in-training, the guards came from everywhere and were found because they had some kind of innate gift, only for them it was a gift for . . .

being an Avalon guard.

I suddenly realized that I had to pee. Badly. I could barely hold it in, and I couldn't go anywhere. I knew I would regret it, but I moved over to Anna and gently shook her awake. Surprisingly, she didn't give me any grief.

"I need to get this soot off," she said, looking down at her hands and clothes, which were still black from the fire incident.

"You bathe, I'll pee."

Khalid appeared from the trees with a small meal of berries he'd found. When he saw that we were both awake, he led us down to the stream, then left us alone for privacy.

Anna cleaned herself, yelping from the cold water with each splash and scrub, while I relieved myself.

Freshly dressed and with bellies full of berries, we finally left for Camelot.

By midday, we came to the edge of the forest. Camelot was still nearly a mile away, but it towered like a mountain before us.

"It's enormous," I said aloud, though I hadn't meant to.

"Actually, it's not that big," Anna said. "Camelot was built for easy protection, not for showing off wealth." And there it was again. Superior Anna showing off her privilege.

"Well, it's the biggest fortress I've ever seen, so excuse my peasantness," I said, then ran down the hill into the rolling fields of grass. I nearly tripped when the bond pulled hard between us, but I couldn't keep the grin from my face upon hearing Anna grunt and tumble. "Oops. I forgot."

"Right," she said. "I'm fine, thanks," she continued, no doubt because of Khalid, who was probably ready with a hand the moment she lost her balance. She stomped past me. I wasn't going to let her do that back to me, so I caught up with her. She snapped, "If you try anything in front of King—"

"You can embarrass yourself just fine, Anna." I stared straight ahead, growing more excited the closer we got to Camelot. I was going to learn from Merlin. Merlin! At Camelot! Before Arthur became king, Camelot was already legendary. As different as we were, Anna and I—all of the priestesses of Avalon—understood that we were alive during a time of history that was so fantastic that future generations would hardly believe it was true. The expression on her face at this very moment was probably the exact same one on mine: total awe.

I tried to memorize every brick of Camelot, both big and small. There was a constant trickle of knights on horseback coming in and going out of the main gates. Someone in a brown robe walked out and across the drawbridge. It was a man with a Roman haircut.

Houdain?

Wow, he was tall. Even at a distance, it was obvious. He scanned the horizon until he spotted us. Then he waved with both arms. As he ran toward us, he tripped on his robe in the grass.

It was adorable.

Quickly bouncing to his feet, he slowed his pace as he headed toward us. When he was a few yards away, he stopped to breathe. "Greetings, priestesses of Avalon!" It came out as more of a wheeze than a strong announcement. "I . . . am Houdain, apprentice to the great Merlin."

Anna spoke first. "We saw you in the mirror."

"Yes. Right. Well." He waited until we were right in front of him, and he stood there with a silly, charming smile on his face.

Anna jabbed me hard in the ribs. I whirled on her. "What?"

"You were about to drool," she said through a particularly sly grin.

I was not about to drool.

Anna glared at me for a long moment before turning back toward Houdain. "I am Priestess Anna, and this is Priestess Bronwyn."

Houdain bowed deeply to each of us. Straightening up again, he said, "Yes."

"And this is Khalid," Anna said with more grace than I'd ever seen from her. "He is an Avalon guard," she announced proudly.

Houdain and Khalid bowed to each other.

Houdain motioned toward Camelot with his arm. "If you would all please follow me." He spun around so fast that his robe billowed out and split to reveal very pale bare legs. For the rest of the hike to Camelot, I stared at his robe. I'd never seen a man's bare legs, except for my father's and brothers', and I couldn't help wanting to see his again.

In no time, we crossed the drawbridge and passed under the towering archway into Camelot. There were covered stands with tradesmen and shops lining each side of the cobblestone road leading to the arched maw of the fortress. The cacophony of sounds hit me all at once. From the clanking of hammers hitting metal at the blacksmith's forge, to the chattering of busy townsfolk strolling up and down the small street, to the yelling of salesmen luring customers in, it was a stark contrast from the peaceful setting of Avalon.

In fact, until Avalon, I had never been near a fortress at all. My village was one of many scattered about the hills and mountains of the far north. I had read about life in court, but no one had written about what else went on inside the walls of a fortress.

As we passed the trade area, Houdain took us in another

direction, where knights practiced their swordplay and the higher classes observed from wooden benches set on top of seven-foot platforms. Being physically above us symbolized their status, and they probably viewed our simple robes as very raggedy compared to theirs. But with a quick glance in their direction, I noticed that no one paid us any attention. I'd expected to at least get some disgusted glances, but we were ignored like we weren't even there.

Houdain stopped at the archway of a pair of large wooden doors guarded by knights on either side. "Priestesses Bronwyn and Anna are here to see the king," Houdain announced.

The knights opened the doors, and we walked inside.

Camelot.

I had always dreamed of coming here, but to be entering into the fortress itself, as personal guests of Merlin? I could barely catch my breath, I was so overwhelmed.

Accompanied by two more guards, Houdain led us forward into the heart of the keep. The stonework had been laid with precision and majesty unlike anything I'd ever seen, almost as if someone had picked out each stone for its uniqueness and beauty. The varying shades of gray made the walls seem like pieces of art.

I barely paid attention to where we were headed, as each new hallway brought new and exciting visuals, from bright and colorful tapestries to hanging wrought iron candelabrums illuminating the darker areas where there were no windows. Everything was a feast for my eyes.

We finally reached another set of arched wooden doors where two more guards stood watch. Houdain introduced us again, and the guards opened the doors wide, revealing a cavern of a room.

The great hall.

Light poured in through the high windows, giving the space

a magical glow. It was so tall that birds of all kinds flew around the ceiling without fear that even the longest pole might swat them away. More intricately woven tapestries hung from the walls, each depicting peaceful settings, from musicians playing their instruments, to towering pine trees, to animals ranging from stags to little bunnies to sheep. Ornately carved benches were placed throughout the room, but a few lined either side of a long dark red carpet leading to a raised platform in the center of the room.

On the platform directly in front of us were King Arthur and Queen Guinevere, sitting on simple high-backed oak chairs. Next to Arthur was Merlin. He was dressed as simply as we were, except his robe was dark and covered by a long chain mail vest. From across the room, his bright blue-violet eyes were on us. Every muscle in my body begged me to turn around and run.

My body jerked forward. Anna was several steps ahead, glaring at me. "Come on," she hissed quietly.

Khalid was at my side, his hand on my elbow. "Are you all right, Priestess Bronwyn?"

I nodded and forced myself to walk forward. Every step was like moving through deep wet snow. Anna walked proudly, though her hands were clasped tightly behind her. Her knuckles were white, and it was a small comfort knowing she was nervous too.

Merlin's expression perplexed me. Did he hate me already? Did he know how unworthy I was to be here? If only he would stop staring at us. *Please stop looking at us*, I said in my head. But Merlin's eyes stayed trained on us. All he did was blink on occasion.

"Your Majesty," Houdain said eagerly, "may I present Priestess Bronwyn and Priestess Anna and their guard, Khalid, of Avalon."

Houdain retreated to stand behind Merlin, and Anna and I were suddenly alone. There was nothing between us and the high king and queen of Britain.

From the corner of my eye, I noticed Anna start to curtsy, so I made myself do the same. I forced my attention to Arthur and Guinevere. I may never have been to court before, but I'd been taught how to behave properly by Priestess Florette. I represented Avalon, and I didn't want to embarrass the island. I wished I had Anna's ability to feign calmness.

Queen Guinevere stood and stepped down toward us. She was beautiful and graceful in every way. Her skin was so smooth it looked as if she'd never worked a hard day in her life. She was shorter than me. So far, everyone in Camelot, except for Houdain, was shorter than me. "Welcome to Camelot," she said in all sincerity. She examined us each in turn, including Khalid, an eyebrow raised a little before she said, "All of you." I wondered if Anna noticed that. Of course, it was difficult *not* to notice how handsome Khalid was, so she couldn't very well blame the queen of Britain for taking note. "We are honored to have two priestesses of Avalon with us."

"We're only in training, Your Majesty," Anna said.

I could hardly think of anything to say.

That was until I was addressed directly.

By Merlin.

Himself.

"Priestess Bronwyn, have you nothing to say?"

I looked at Merlin. Houdain was right beside him, and his head slightly swung from Merlin to me and back again.

"I'm . . . happy to finally be here?" Was that really a question? I wanted to hide!

Anna's jaw slackened. I was blowing it.

"It was a long journey from Avalon, sir, but I am looking forward to every experience here at Camelot." I must have recovered well because Houdain grinned at me.

Merlin whispered into Arthur's ear, and then the king stood and stepped down to us. He was muscular and strong, which wasn't surprising given he was a great knight himself. He reached out for my hand and held it in his, and I felt my face flushing. "Camelot is at your disposal, Priestess Bronwyn."

Arthur took Anna's hand next and spoke to her. I have no idea what they said. My mind reeled. Khalid's hand on my elbow steadied me again. Thankfully, he was being subtle. I scolded myself for being overwhelmed. I'd been through hard times, frightening times, dangerous times. This was none of those things, surely. Why was I acting as if I were some little girl with no life experiences?

Houdain came back to us as Arthur and Guinevere returned to their chairs. He grinned at me again. He grinned a lot. It made me feel better. "I'll take you to your quarters. You'll each have your own room."

"We just need one," Anna said. "We're bound together."

"Bound?" Houdain asked. "You mean, like, you can't be apart from each other?"

"How else would you interpret *bound*?" I asked him.

Houdain frowned and nodded his head. "Point taken." We followed him out of the room, and as the two big doors closed again, he asked, "Does that mean you two have to do everything together?"

"I guess," I said. "Why?"

Houdain's face paled when he said, "What about things like . . . bathing?"

"Camelot is beautiful," Khalid said suddenly. "Do you agree, Priestess Anna?"

"Um," she said.

"Priestess Bronwyn? Have you ever seen such beauty?" Khalid said.

"N-no, Khalid," I stammered. Were we making idle chitchat?

"Master Houdain," Khalid continued, "is it possible for me to have a small room near the priestesses' quarters?"

"Uh, yes," Houdain replied. "There's a room off of their quarters for you." There was a long silence as we wound our way up a long staircase and into a hallway. He stopped at another pair of double doors, though these were far less spectacular, just simple wood with rounded wrought iron handles and decorative hinges. "This is you." He opened the doors. Anna and I stepped inside.

Houdain said to Khalid, "Any time you want a break, I'm happy to stay here to watch the priestesses. To make sure Priestess Bronwyn—and Priestess Anna, of course—are, you know, safe and all."

"That will be unnecessary, but thank you, Master Houdain," Khalid said.

Nodding to a door a few yards away, Houdain said, "That's the door to your room, Khalid."

Khalid nodded his thanks but stayed put in the doorway.

As we walked farther into our room, Houdain waved and called out, "If you need anything, I'm your man!" He stumbled away as if in a daze.

After he was out of view, Khalid bowed slightly to us. "Priestesses," Khalid said, "I will leave you now."

Anna practically ran back to the doors and up to Khalid. Fortunately, I was paying attention, or she would have pulled me off-balance.

"Where are you going?" she asked.

"Never far, Priestess Anna."

"He's giving us some privacy, dummy," I said. "Thank you, Khalid." I closed the doors as he stepped out of view.

"That was rude," Anna growled.

"You can't take a hint."

"What hint? He was trying not to embarrass me, unlike you." Anna stomped across the room, and again I had to move with her.

The room was comfortable yet exquisitely decorated. In fact, it wasn't until that very moment that I noticed how beautiful everything was. It was meant for royalty. There were furs on the floor and bed, and the fire in the hearth took the chill from the air. Tapestries covered the walls, each with unique artwork, from battles, to jousting, to a lovely one of a horse and foal.

"Is there another bed?" Anna asked with a furrowed eyebrow. "I thought we'd have two."

"Maybe that door leads to another bedroom." I nodded toward the one closed door on the far wall. "It might be close enough with our bond."

"You don't think that's Khalid's room, do you?" Anna asked with an excited crack in her voice.

Shaking my head, I said, "His room is on the opposite side of that one."

With a disappointed sigh and slump of her shoulders, Anna hurried to the mysterious door and opened it while I stood by the bed in our main room.

Sure enough, there was another four-poster bed inside.

We both sighed in relief, and Anna walked toward it.

I was yanked forward, pulled well past the bed and almost into the second room.

Anna hadn't reached the other bed yet.

Our bond wouldn't even let us have separate sleeping areas.

My heart sank. "We're going to have to share."

"I need privacy," she said, hands on her hips, shocked at the turn of events.

"You should have thought of that before you stole my scrying stone."

"It wasn't *your* stone!"

"It was assigned to me. Therefore, it *was* mine."

"And how was I supposed to know that *this* would be the result of *that*?" Anna was nearly shrieking at me, and she slammed the door to the second room as if it had attacked her.

I was tired of her thinking that she could decide my fate. Every time I wanted to move, I had to either wait for her or catch her off guard. I wanted this settled before we interacted with anyone else at Camelot. She would not be in charge of me.

"You wanted the scrying stone when you wanted it, so you took it when you wanted to take it. You want a room for yourself? Then what? I'm supposed to hang out on the floor so you can have comfort? It's not about you, Anna. I'd be happy to show you how much it's not about you."

"What are you going to do, Bronwyn? Toss me across the room with a ball of light again? Go ahead! You'll burn Camelot to the ground in the process. I know this isn't about me. It's always about *you*. 'Poor Bronwyn. It's okay you demolished Camelot. You couldn't help yourself.' You can do no wrong!"

My blood boiled, and my skin burned. Magic welled up in my hands. As furious as I was, I screamed in my head not to lose control. As blind as Anna was to the bigger picture, she had experienced the consequences of my uncontrolled magic firsthand.

Not knowing what else to do, I covered my ears with my hands and stomped away. In my head, I sang something my mother used to sing to me as a child to block out Anna's voice. I lurched toward a far window, feeling Anna attempt to stop our bond from making her move, but I was bigger and stronger than her. I took one hard step forward, and Anna must have lost her balance because I made it the rest of the way to the window without effort.

I leaned against the wall next to the window and peered out. We were a hundred feet up, and I could easily see the forests and hills for miles.

Anna grabbed my hands from my ears.

Deafening sounds pierced my head like knives. Falling to my knees from the pain, I covered my ears again.

"Bronwyn!" Anna yelled, but I only knew it because I read her lips. Sounds invaded my ears, my hands barely muffling the noise.

Two pairs of hands grabbed ahold of me. One pair was larger and firmer than the other. I opened my eyes to see Khalid's face near mine. "Breathe," he said calmly. "Breathe."

I took deep breaths, my eyes shifting back and forth between Khalid and Anna. Slowly, the noise faded, but everything was still very loud. I took my hands from my ears.

"What happened?" Anna asked, but it was like she was still screaming at me.

"Not so loud!" I said. My own voice was too loud. I said it again in a whisper, but even that was like thunder. "I think," I whispered, "I cast a spell on myself."

Khalid helped me to my feet. I leaned against the window again, letting the chilly breeze cool me. The shock of it was colder than I had expected, as I was now drenched in sweat.

Anna leaned in, eyebrows drawn together. "It'll wear off soon, right?"

"It's already starting to," I said.

I heard a man's voice say in a hissing whisper, "He would never believe you."

I searched the room. It was just me, Anna, and Khalid, and that was definitely not Khalid's voice.

Another man hissed back, "I would give my life for him to see the truth about you."

The first man laughed quietly. "You will die for nothing, Gawain. My father sees and believes what he wants to."

I leaned out the window, following the voices.

"What is it?" Anna asked, leaning out next to me.

On the ground below us stood two men. One wore the armor of the Knights of the Round Table. The other was a nobleman in dark clothes. They stood face-to-face. I couldn't see their faces though. There was no one else around.

The nobleman tapped the knight's chain mail and said, "When Arthur dies and I become high king, I'll build you a memorial."

Mordred! The nobleman was King Arthur's son. We'd read about him in our Avalon studies. He began to walk away, but the knight, Sir Gawain, grabbed him by the arm. "I should strike you down—"

"And break your king's heart?"

"A heart that would continue beating."

Mordred yanked his arm away and straightened his clothes. "You're too good to strike down an unarmed opponent." Mordred backed away from Sir Gawain and said a little louder, "And that *is* your biggest weakness." He turned and walked away. Sir Gawain stood there for a moment before rushing off.

I straightened up again. "I need to sit down." The sounds around me were beginning to quiet down to normal.

Anna walked with me to a large sofa, and we sat down on its

blue velvet cushions. "What were you looking at?"

"I was listening. I could hear them."

"Those two men on the ground? That's incredible."

"It was horrible, Anna. Mordred. The king's son. He wants to kill the king!"

Chapter 7
ANNA

Mordred? If I recalled from one of our monarchy classes in Avalon, he was Arthur's *illegitimate* son, but I didn't remember anything nefarious about the man aside from that. "Wants? Or *plans*?" It was a big difference to me. People could *want* to kill the king, but the reality that they were *planning* on it was usually just talk. Wanting to kill or remove nobility was more common than most people would think. It was caused by all sorts of things: jealously or thinking they could do better, for instance. I used to hear minor houses talk about overthrowing our duke all the time, fantasizing about "accidents" and such.

I knew Bronwyn hadn't been exposed to any kind of nobility, so what she might've thought was a threat could've simply been a jealous son fantasizing about being king one day. It would be hard growing up with a father like King Arthur, the man who was a hero to all of England. How could Mordred ever measure up? No wonder he talked of removing his father; he'd never be as beloved as his dad. In fact, the more I thought about it, the more I was certain Bronwyn had heard wrong. She'd probably misunderstood the conversation completely.

Bronwyn finally answered my question. "*Plans*. Do you think I'm such an idiot that I can't tell the difference?" She yelled that last bit, so I assumed her little superhearing spell mishap was finally over.

"Okay, then what was the plan?" I said a little too rudely. I didn't like showing this side of myself in front of Khalid, but Bronwyn was like a bug I couldn't swat.

Bronwyn paused, thinking, then huffed as she stood up from the couch. "He didn't say. Mordred was arguing with a knight. Gawain, he called him. Sir Gawain said that he wished Arthur could see Mordred for who he really was and threatened to kill Mordred, and then Mordred said Gawain would have died for nothing and that after he killed his father he'd build Gawain a memorial . . ." Bronwyn trailed off of her rant. "I know it doesn't sound that dire, but I'm telling you, something about Mordred scared me."

"Scared?" My interest was piqued. Usually noblemen were stuffy babies; one that scared the almighty Bronwyn intrigued me.

Bronwyn wasn't ashamed to admit her fears, and she nodded. "Anna, I think he knows magic. I could sense it. At least I think I could sense it. I don't know. It's like waking up from a nightmare: at first you're terrified, then the more you think it through, the less threatening it becomes." She plopped down on the couch with a sigh. "I'm overreacting, aren't I?"

Did she want my opinion, or was she rationalizing out loud to herself? If I picked wrong, she'd bite my head off. I chose to be diplomatic. "No. Priestesses Elaine and Florette wanted us to trust our instincts. If your instincts tell you Arthur's son is dangerous, then I think we should investigate. Maybe we should tell Merlin, or ask him anyway? He may have more insight on Mordred than what we learned in Avalon. If anyone would know Mordred is a magic user, it would be Merlin, right?" I tried to be helpful. I actually wasn't all that concerned about Arthur's son. My honest opinion was that Bronwyn's spell-gone-wrong had enhanced *all* her senses, including her sense of danger and fear. It had probably felt very real to Bronwyn, but I could be the voice of reason.

Bronwyn shook her head. "I don't want to tell Merlin. I don't want to tell anyone." Then she eyed Khalid, who had all but disappeared during the conversation. "You won't tell anyone, will you?"

Khalid bowed slightly. "You two are my charges. I do as you ask. The only authority higher than you two are High Priestesses Florette and Elaine."

Relief flooded Bronwyn's face. "Good." Then she turned back to me. "Can we follow Mordred? If we find anything, *then* we'll tell someone."

I should have agreed and been done with it, but I wanted her to hear my suspicions first. "Now, don't get mad at me, but do you think that maybe when your hearing was amplified so were your emotions? Like fear or paranoia?"

Surprisingly, Bronwyn didn't jump to anger. "Maybe. The more time that passes, the calmer I get." She sighed. "Can we please follow him, just to make sure?"

"Fine, as long as you're willing to admit you may have been wrong if Mordred ends up being what I think he is: a spoiled prince who wants his daddy's throne."

I had met our duke's firstborn son, Balin, before leaving for Avalon. I was only six, but even back then I'd been able to tell what a rich, entitled brat he was. I was pretty sure we'd find out Mordred was no different.

"Trust me, I would be thrilled to be wrong. We're supposed to be learning magic from Merlin, not foiling assassination attempts." Bronwyn appeared as if she wanted to be mistaken, which made me relax a little.

"I will come with you," Khalid announced.

Bronwyn shook her head. "You don't have to, Khalid. We'll follow Mordred at a distance. Hopefully Anna is right and it's nothing."

"I *will* be coming with you." Khalid left no room for argument. A thrill of excitement rushed through me.

Khalid walked to the doorway, opened it, and stepped outside, waiting for us to proceed. He wasn't messing around. Wherever we went, he went, which was perfectly fine by me.

"Don't get too excited," Bronwyn whispered out of his earshot. "The way he looked at Queen Guinevere . . . I think he's in love."

"*She* was the one drooling all over him; his face didn't even move!" I whispered harshly so that Khalid couldn't hear the sudden high pitch of my voice. My heart sank. Queen Guinevere appreciating Khalid's beauty had made my heart squeeze with jealousy. Of course, she was King Arthur's wife, but I was more worried about what *Khalid* thought of *her*, not the other way around.

From Bronwyn's satisfied smile, I could tell she was enjoying my discomfort. She whispered, "Well, at least you know he likes blondes, right?"

I kept my voice as quiet as possible. "If Khalid harbors any crush on Queen Guinevere, then I don't have a chance at all. She's the most beautiful woman in England, and I'm, well . . . *me*."

Before Bronwyn could insult me more, I pushed my way forward. "Let's get this over with."

Bronwyn didn't argue. She kept a sly grin on her face, and I wanted to punch it off her. As if I weren't already humiliated when it came to Khalid. The poor man must've regretted his decision to guard us.

As we joined him in the hallway outside our room, I avoided eye contact with him. Walking forward, I moved fast so I could hear the small grunt from Bronwyn as I tugged on our bond, causing her to trip slightly as she exited the room.

Catching up to me, Bronwyn kept pace. "Do you know where you're going?"

"Not really, but I figured we'd head in the direction Mordred went," I answered.

"But we're five floors up from where he was."

"They're called stairs." I tried to keep the sarcasm out of my voice but failed miserably.

"Right." Bronwyn sounded unsure. "Okay, you lead then."

I didn't answer and simply moved forward toward where I assumed the stairs to be. The evenly spaced stones, which varied in shape and size, from the size of my palm to the size of a loaf of bread, felt smooth and cold on my slippered feet. But there was method to the madness, a pattern in the chaos. It was stonework craftsmanship at its finest. Iron sconces holding large candles hung on the stacked stone walls, though their flames had been extinguished in exchange for the morning light that poured in through the high windows in each hallway. It surprised me how most fortresses and keeps were built so similarly. I had only been to a few before leaving for Avalon, but all of them had staircases in the northwestern corners.

Sure enough, a spiral staircase built into the wall opened up before us. I acted more confident than I felt as I descended the winding stone steps that led deeper into the fortress. After we reached the bottom floor, I stopped.

"Should we search the main rooms on this floor through those arches?" I asked. "We also have to consider he may have headed upstairs, downstairs, or walked through those doors over there that lead outside."

Bronwyn nodded toward the archway. "Let's try this level first."

I let her lead this time, keeping my eye on Khalid, who stayed at least twenty feet behind us. I sometimes wondered if the guards of Avalon used magic to blend into the walls; there were several times I thought we had lost him.

Following Bronwyn through the arches, I felt the rough textured stone beneath me, unlike the smoother floors of the stairs and the hallway above. I'd need to wear thicker stockings or I'd stub a toe—that, or my feet would freeze off. I ignored my discomfort and eyed each person we passed for any signs of Mordred.

Not that I knew what Mordred looked like. We were searching for what we remembered him wearing at this point. But the longer we walked, the more I wanted to go back to our room, sit by the cozy fire, and read a good book. I made a mental note to ask Houdain if I could borrow a few tomes from the library, maybe even have Merlin recommend a few. The thought brought me a wave of anticipation. Though I missed the island of Avalon, being in Camelot and learning from the greatest magician of our time was exhilarating.

Of course, an hour into arriving we were already on a wild-goose chase because of Bronwyn's failure to control her magic. It was a bigger problem than I had ever imagined. I needed to stop provoking her before she accidently used her magic to toss me out the window.

"Ladies?"

I whirled around to see Houdain, who was staring at Bronwyn with wide-eyed wonder.

Bronwyn stopped and smiled awkwardly at Houdain. Was that how I looked when I greeted Khalid? I hoped not.

"Oh, hello, Houdain," Bronwyn sputtered.

"What are you two up to? Exploring Camelot? I can take you on a tour if you'd like." Houdain might as well have been panting. "I'm surprised Khalid let you venture alone. He seems very protective." He winked. "A little too protective if you ask me." He was trying to be funny but failing miserably.

"Master Houdain," Khalid said.

Houdain practically jumped out of his skin, his face going pale. "O-oh, hi, Khalid, didn't see you there. You're really good at your job." Then Houdain turned back to Bronwyn. "So? Tour?"

I decided to step in and get to the point. "Houdain, we're trying to find Mordred. Do you know where he is?"

Houdain's eyebrows lifted dramatically. "The king's son? Why do you need to find him?"

"We simply want to clear up a misunderstanding is all." I smiled as disarmingly as I could. "Can you help us?"

"Uh, sure," Houdain said, though he didn't seem sure at all. I couldn't tell if it was because he was trying to figure out what our intentions were or if he didn't want to have anything to do with Mordred. "I passed him in the lower hall a few moments ago. He should still be there."

When Bronwyn's face lit up, Houdain lost all hesitation.

He held out his arms for both of us to take. Bronwyn took his right arm shyly. I wasn't about to take Houdain's other arm, but when Bronwyn gave me a please-don't-make-me-be-the-only-one-taking-his-arm look, I grudgingly placed my arm through his left arm. I just hoped Khalid didn't think I liked Houdain. Not that it mattered. Khalid would never see me as anything more than his charge.

Walking through a few more corridors, we entered a giant room lined with even more hanging tapestries. Fortresses were full of them, but it was always interesting to observe what each room's theme was. This one was hunting, as all the tapestries were either of the hunt itself, with hounds and horses racing toward the forest, or of deer running through forests or meadows. Light poured in from the arched windows above, making shapes on the stone floor. About half a dozen people stood in three different groups, talking and enjoying one another's company. Ornate wooden benches were scattered throughout, just like in the great hall.

"He's over there, talking to Duke Ellington and Sir Helford." Houdain motioned with his head.

To Houdain's disappointment, I took my arm out of his, as did Bronwyn.

I could only see the back of Mordred's head, so it was impossible to gauge an opinion on whether or not he was a king slayer. He laughed with his two companions and seemed quite normal from behind.

Bronwyn appeared to agree because she sighed, saying, "I'm insane. It must have been the spell. We should probably go."

"I think that's a good idea," I said.

Then Mordred turned around, and I could see his face clearly. My heart stopped.

It was *him*.

The man from the scrying stone.

The man who terrified me.

The man who'd been able to *see* me *through* the scrying stone.

The man who knew magic.

In that moment, I was certain what Bronwyn had overhead was the absolute truth: Mordred planned to kill the king.

"What?" Bronwyn stared at me. "I know that look. It's your petrified look. Did you see him do something? What?"

I whirled on her. "Calm down!" My heart pounded in my chest. *I should follow my own advice!* "I saw Mordred in the scrying stone back at Avalon, though I didn't know who he was then. I sensed he had power, and as soon as I did, he stared at me *through* the scrying stone!"

Houdain shook his head. "Mordred? Magical? I don't think so. Master Merlin would be able to detect that."

I ignored Houdain. I knew what I'd witnessed, and I was sure of one thing: Mordred was a magician. And he wasn't a good person. Not at all.

Bronwyn and I were on the same page for once. She nodded to me, quietly asking, "We following him?"

"Definitely," I answered.

Houdain's face paled in panic. "Wait, what? We can't follow the king's son!"

I turned to Houdain. "You can do whatever you like. We have reason to believe that Mordred will attempt to kill his father, and we're not going to sit idly by while that happens. Not if we can do something about it."

Khalid walked up beside me. "He's on the move."

Khalid was right. Mordred had left the two men and was

headed toward the hallway beyond.

Not caring whether Houdain came with us or not, Bronwyn and I walked as fast as possible without appearing as if we were racing to follow Mordred.

Arriving at the corridor Mordred had gone through, we caught the tail end of him rounding a corner. The candles on the sconces burned brightly, casting the remnants of Mordred's shadow on the stone floor, though he was no longer in view.

We trailed him at a distance for quite a while. He'd turn a corner, then we'd walk down the hallway ourselves, always knowing which direction he turned by the shadows on the ground. We were headed into the bowels of the fortress now. Candles were replaced with torches, and the fire gave off heat as we passed each one. Khalid remained behind us and out of our sight, but I knew he'd be there to fight if we needed him. I hoped we wouldn't have to attack the *king's* son. But if we did, Khalid was the man I'd want for the job.

Houdain tagged along for the ride, scared but unwilling to let us go alone. He kept muttering things like, "I'll just say I was giving them a tour," and "You know girls, they like to explore." Bronwyn had to shush him several times for fear of Mordred catching us.

We rounded a tight corner and almost stumbled on ourselves as we realized Mordred was only ten feet away, stopped at a large wooden door. Quickly, we slid back behind the corner so Mordred wouldn't see us. In Bronwyn's haste to hide herself, she shoved me, and I toppled backward. Typical.

But to my surprise, Khalid's hands were quick as he wrapped them around me from behind, pulling me away from a torch that had nearly set my hair ablaze. "Careful, Priestess Anna." His voice was a whisper, his lips pressed against my ear.

I couldn't tell if I was sweating from the heat of the flame, from Khalid's touch, or from his lips being that close to me. My breath caught in my throat as I struggled to function with any kind of normalcy. "Thank you," I whispered.

A loud clank jolted us out of the moment, and Khalid's arms were no longer around me. I ached for him to hold me again, physically feeling the absence of his warmth.

Bronwyn, completely unaware that she had almost lit me on fire, quickly peered around the corner. "Mordred went through that door. What room is that?" she asked Houdain.

Houdain obviously hadn't expected his day to go like this, but I had to give him credit, as he didn't run and hide. "Uh, it's Master Merlin's potion room." He went from nervous about being caught to nervous about why Mordred would need to be in one of Merlin's rooms. "Mordred must be trying to find Master Merlin. I should go get him."

I shook my head. "*Or* he's up to something treacherous involving the king."

"Listen, Houdain, I heard Mordred tell a knight named Gawain that he planned on killing his father. That's why we've been following him. Are you going to help us or what?" Bronwyn had hope in her eyes as she asked Houdain. She wanted him to be on our team and not run and tell his master what we were up to.

Houdain swallowed hard. "Mordred actually said he was going to kill the king?"

Bronwyn nodded solemnly. "Yes. Now, Anna and I were sent to Camelot for a reason, and maybe this is it. Maybe we're supposed to save King Arthur."

A surge of inspiration filled my body at that sentiment. And Bronwyn might be right; maybe that *was* the reason fate had brought us to Camelot. The Goddess worked her magic in mysterious ways.

"If we could just know for sure what he's doing in there," Bronwyn said, frustrated.

"What about that spell you accidently cast on yourself? If I could channel that into a seer spell . . ." I let Bronwyn's imagination connect the dots.

"We could see through the wall," she exclaimed excitedly. Then her face fell. "I don't know how to control it. I don't even know how I cast it."

It was so frustrating knowing how much power Bronwyn had and that she had no control over it. I was a master at control. If I'd had an ounce of her raw magic, I could've rivaled Merlin. Well, probably not, but the point was Bronwyn had so much potential.

"Maybe if I cast a binding spell on top of the seer spell, it would rein in your power so you couldn't accidentally blow up Camelot," I said.

Houdain's eye grew round. "Blow up Camelot?"

"I was exaggerating." I wasn't, but no sense in scaring the boy any more than we already had.

Bronwyn nodded. "Let's try it." She set her jaw in determination.

I grabbed her hands and clasped them tightly. "I'm going to cast both spells, and you try and recreate what you did in our bedroom."

Hands shaking, Bronwyn nodded.

I began speaking the words of the spells, weaving the two together, both seer and binding, feeling Bronwyn's energy.

Bronwyn closed her eyes, and I could see she was concentrating. No.

I could *feel* it.

I nearly stopped breathing. I could see a piece of Bronwyn's innate magic. It was blinding, like staring into the sun.

I kept reciting the words of the seer and binding spells, trying to hold back her power from destroying anything in her path. My eyes began to burn. My hands began to burn. I couldn't let go.

She's going to kill me.

Khalid grabbed my hands and pried them from Bronwyn's. The pain seared my blood as if fire were pumping through my veins. My hands were bright red.

"Priestess Anna, are you all right?" Khalid's eyes were wide and full of concern. It made me want to burst. Why did I always have to get hurt to get his attention? It didn't matter. I'd take it.

"Anna, I'm so sorry. I didn't . . ." Bronwyn took a shuddering breath.

"Ladies, look." Houdain's voice was tinged with awe.

When I turned to see what he was referring to, my mouth dropped in shock.

We had done it.

The stone wall in front of us appeared as if we had cut a hole in it, but upon touch, it was still solid. We had made it invisible.

Mordred stood at a table using a pestle to smash something in a clay bowl. Not knowing the ingredients, it was hard to tell what he was making.

Houdain stared in disbelief, then he said, "He's using hemlock. It's poison. It would kill anyone who ingested it."

Mordred pulled out a jeweled cup and placed it on the table.

Houdain whispered with a slight shrill, "That's King Arthur's cup."

We all watched in horror as Mordred poured the poison into his father's cup.

"Okay, now we go get Merlin." I gulped.

Chapter 8
BRONWYN

Mordred cleaned out the clay bowl and placed the hemlock bottle back on the shelf. Lifting the poisoned cup, he turned to leave. A devious grin spread across his face as his eyes swept across the wall we stared through.

"He's not going to hold on to that for long," I said. "We don't have time to get Merlin."

We hurried back down the corridor and rounded the corner. The clank of the door opening, followed by the thud of it closing, made my heart race. Mordred's footfalls grew closer. He was going the way he had come, and we were in the way! We practically ran back through the twists and turns of the hallways we'd followed him through, finally arriving at the main corridor. Entering the dining hall, we had to weave through a crowd of nobles gathering for dinner. There were at least fifty people, which instantly caused my stomach to flutter. Too many people.

Five long wooden tables were spaced in parallel rows. The

tables were more rustic, but the wooden benches on either side were intricately carved. The only chair in the room was King Arthur's, which was placed at the end of the middle table. Most of the people milled about the room, talking about whatever it was nobles talked about. Anna knew more about that than I did.

Scanning the room, I tried to locate King Arthur and finally found him conferring with a small group of people near the middle of the room, not yet to the table. We had to get to him before Mordred could deliver his deadly potion.

"What do we do?" Anna asked. "Can we grab the cup from Mordred directly?"

"Why not?" I said. "We'll wait for Mordred to hand the cup to the king or put it on the table, then grab it. We need King Arthur to see Mordred with the murder weapon or he might not believe us."

"Right." Anna swallowed hard. "Are we ready for this?"

I nodded, and my chest tightened from nerves.

"I'll try to find Master Merlin," Houdain announced. "I'll tell him what's happening." He started away, then turned back briefly to say, "Be careful."

We were about to cause some serious drama in Camelot. That didn't bother me though. We were doing the right thing. What bothered me was that a son would want to kill his father.

Mordred strolled into the dining hall, slowly making his way to King Arthur's table. Arthur was still making his rounds, speaking to more guests.

Mordred took the cup from underneath his cloak and placed it on the table.

Anna and I ran across the room toward Mordred. We yelled, "*Stop!*" at the same time, drawing everyone's attention.

The room hushed to shocked silence as we pointed at Mordred and approached. I grabbed the cup from him and peered down; mead was already inside.

"What is this?" asked King Arthur as he walked through the parting crowd.

"There's poison in here, my lord," I said, holding the cup out to him.

Arthur's gaze moved from me to Anna to Mordred. His eyes finally rested on his son, but he addressed us. "How do you know?"

Anna said, "We witnessed Mordred. He broke into Merlin's potion room. He had your cup with him, my lord, and he put hemlock into it. It's a deadly herb."

Arthur held out his hand, and I gave him the cup. He glanced inside, smelled it, and then handed it to Mordred. "Poison, Son?"

"I am many things to you, Father, but never your murderer." With that, he put the cup to his lips and drank the mead entirely.

Nothing happened.

Anna and I exchanged incredulous glances.

Mordred tilted the cup toward Arthur and then us, showing that the cup was empty.

He grinned.

Arthur turned toward Anna and me, not at all happy but remaining calm and regal. "Priestess Bronwyn, Priestess Anna, you are here as guests with the intention of training to become great leaders of your people. You are not here *to spy*." The last two words were low and growly.

I lowered my head and wanted to scream, *People can build tolerances to poisonous herbs! Check the cup for signs that the hemlock was there at all!* But that wasn't going to happen. We were strangers accusing his only son of attempted murder with no proof other than our words.

Houdain had arrived, but Merlin wasn't with him. And from the way he shifted nervously from foot to foot, I could tell that he recognized Arthur's disbelief and anger. If only Merlin were here.

Arthur turned to Houdain with a nod. No words were spoken, but it was clear that Arthur was handing us over to our master's apprentice. Houdain motioned for us to come. Anna and I both shot Mordred a knowing look.

He simply blinked at us.

As we left the dining hall, Arthur called out to his guests to join him at the tables for the feast.

We followed Houdain in silence until we were outside in a courtyard. Houdain led us toward a garden that seemed as big as Avalon itself. It was also nearly as beautiful, with greenery perfectly trimmed against the four walls of the courtyard and flowers of every color. From the moisture of the plants, moss had grown on the grout between the stones and climbed its way up the surrounding walls, along with several vines.

Houdain's eyes were wide, and he had to clasp his hands together to steady them. "That was . . . scary."

Exactly. That was very scary.

"Mordred had to have built up a tolerance for hemlock," Anna said. "He must have been planning this for a long time."

Houdain said, "Or he's paranoid someone would try killing him instead. I tried to find Merlin, but I couldn't. We need to tell him. Maybe he'll be able to convince Arthur of the danger."

"But if the king won't listen to us *or* Merlin, we'll have to prove Mordred's guilt somehow," I said. "You know Mordred's going to keep trying."

"We'll have to keep following him," Anna said.

"Why don't we do a spell to reveal his intentions?" I suggested.

"We can't use magic, Bronwyn. A lot of people don't trust it."

"What do you mean? Magic is natural. Nature doesn't lie."

"Not at court," she said. "Say we did find something out with a spell. Arthur could accuse us of creating a spell that revealed what we wanted it to reveal. Like we made it up."

"That's stupid," I said.

Anna's face scrunched.

"I don't mean *you're* stupid. I mean anyone who doesn't trust magic is . . . ridiculous!" I clarified.

Anna's face softened a little.

"Well, people can be ridiculous," she said, still a little huffy.

"Magic is our best bet," I said as the setting sun's glow illuminated the garden with dazzling reds and oranges. It really was beautiful. "This is a marvelous place, Houdain." My eyes searched for his, but he'd been staring at me the whole time.

"It's . . . q-quiet," he stammered.

Did he *like* me? *Why* would he like me though? I was a plain peasant in priestess's clothing and an explosion waiting to happen. If he *did* like me, then the feelings I was already having for him would get stronger and I would do something stupid . . . or worse. Anger wasn't the only emotion that set my powers off. Any strong emotion that made me forget to concentrate did the trick.

When I turned ten years old, my father bought me a brand-new tunic. No one else had ever worn it before, and there weren't any patches or marks on it. I was so excited to put it on that I tore it in half with my mind. I was devastated, thinking I had broken my parents' hearts. They must have traded so much to get it. My mother sewed it right up though, and no one could even tell what I'd done. But *I* knew. I hardly ever wore it because I was afraid to ruin it.

The more my powers grew, the less I spent time with people. I was eager to go to Avalon, not only because I would learn how to control my powers, but because I thought that being around strangers would save me from myself. I didn't need to get close to anyone. But then I met Anna, and she made me feel like I didn't belong, and my emotions went haywire. I never had the chance to start learning control. My powers kept growing, and I kept finding myself unable to distance from people.

And now Houdain. If he did like me, he'd back off soon enough when he saw the *real* me. Because in the end, there was nothing about me that was worthy of being liked, especially by someone like Houdain. He was tall, adorable, and in control of himself.

I wished I could read his thoughts by staring into his dark eyes.

"Ridiculous," I repeated.

"What is?" Anna asked.

"This . . . whole thing," I said, pushing my feelings aside. "First of all, the king should believe us. We're priestesses of Avalon, right? Aren't we supposed to be trusted? One of us will be advisor to the court someday, just like Priestess Elaine."

"We can't forget that we're still priestesses-in-training, Bronwyn," Anna said. "We're only guests, and not even guests of the court. We're Merlin's guests. We need physical evidence to present to the king."

"Are you suggesting we break into Mordred's room or something?"

"Of course not!" Anna snapped. "But we can't very well use your magic."

"You can do incantations just fine," I snapped back. "I'm sure there's some kind of spying spell in that advanced mind of yours. Don't you have a whole library in there?"

"We should talk to Priestesses Florette and Elaine," Anna said.

"I agree."

"Good. Let's get back to our room then." Anna didn't wait for me to answer and started back toward the garden opening.

I was about to follow when Houdain touched my arm. I turned toward him.

"You should see this place when it's fully night," he said.

The bond between Anna and me reached its limit, and I was tugged off-balance. He caught me.

"Wouldn't it be too dark to see anything?" I asked, forcing my mind to be logical and distant.

"Well, yes, but when the moon is full, it's a whole different thing."

"What do you mean?"

"It's like another world," he said. "You kinda have to be here to see it." He shifted his feet, head slightly tilted. "I come out here a lot."

"Life at court must be overwhelming," I said.

I felt a tug.

"Are you coming or what?" Anna yelled from across the courtyard.

"We're coming," I answered back.

Houdain and I walked toward Anna and the exit of the courtyard as he responded to my observation. "Court isn't that overwhelming for me. I'm just an apprentice. It's more that after all these years, I'm still not used to the fortress. There's no green inside."

"But you seem so comfortable here."

He laughed lightly as he touched my elbow, steering me away from a root that had busted through the stone. Through my sleeve, his touch sent shivers through my body.

"I don't think about it," he said. "I'm an apprentice. I'm not expected to do anything but be respectful to the nobles and do whatever Master Merlin says. I don't have to impress anyone. I couldn't even if I tried."

"You impressed me," I said.

"Really?" His eyes lit up.

Those eyes!

My foot caught on a slightly upraised stone, and my face was about to meet the ground.

Houdain caught me before I face-planted on a mossy stone, easily lifting me to my feet.

"Thank you." The magic surged in me at his touch, my emotions too powerful to rein in. I needed to distance myself, at least a little. I gently pulled away from him, though it physically pained me to do so.

We began walking again. I didn't want Anna to yank me into a wall if I stood still.

"Of course. It was nothing," he said, but then his eyes went wide. "I mean, it was something. I'm glad I caught you. I mean, I've always been strong, and you're very light for me, so catching you was easy. You're much lighter than a log."

"Well, that's good," I said, unsure of why he'd compare me to a piece of wood.

"Much, much lighter. And softer. I mean, you're nothing like a log. I was comparing you to a log because I've carried lots of logs and not other women, so the logs were all I had in my incredibly dull mind to compare you to."

"Was that your job?" I asked. "Carrying logs?"

"What? No. Yes. I had to fell trees from time to time. In fact, I helped build my family's house." His chest slightly puffed out in pride. "We used the wood for the hearth as well, or to build chairs, or . . . anything really. We didn't have a lot of coins. We lived by ourselves near Merlin's cave."

Merlin had a cave?

"Merlin has a cave?" Anna asked.

Anna had stopped to let us catch up, Khalid next to her.

"Uh. Yes. He does strong magic there. Not here. Please don't tell anybody."

We swore our secrecy to Houdain, and he relaxed.

He ducked his chin and swallowed hard at having revealed something of his life: that he was even poorer than I was. It made me wish that much more that things were different.

"We should probably go speak with the high priestesses now," I said, and Houdain nodded. "I'd like to see this place at night. If the king doesn't kick us out."

Houdain laughed.

Anna said, "We accused his son of attempted murder. Why wouldn't he kick us out?"

Houdain said, "Because you're priestesses of Avalon. Only Master Merlin could make you leave."

Anna said, "I'm pretty sure if King Arthur tells him to, Merlin will do it."

"Maybe." Houdain shrugged. "But it didn't seem like King

Arthur was angry enough to banish either of you."

Anna and I glanced at each other, and we both added a *yet* to his statement with only our eyes.

Houdain left us at the doors to our room. Khalid was somehow already inside and standing by the windows. I'd never seen him totally relaxed, and I didn't think I ever would. His job was guarding Avalon priestesses, so as long as we held that title, Khalid would always be at attention.

Anna and I sat next to each other in front of a polished copper mirror as she spoke the incantation to call upon a connection with the high priestesses.

Nothing.

"Are you saying it right?" I asked. Seeing Anna's affronted expression, I said, "I simply meant that we've had quite a day and you may have forgotten a few words." I wasn't sure if that helped.

With a huff, Anna spoke through gritted teeth. "I said it to perfection. Something seems to be blocking the spell."

I swallowed hard. "You don't think Mordred . . . ?"

Anna's face paled. "Let me try one more time." She recited the incantation again.

Nothing.

"We should go find Merlin," I said with a slight shake in my voice. This was Mordred's doing. I didn't know how, but I knew it in my bones.

Leaving our room with Khalid close behind, we caught up to Houdain, who had barely made it halfway down the hall. We filled him in on our mission, and he quickly agreed. We all hurried back down to the main floor to search for Merlin. We even went to his potion room, where we had seen Mordred preparing the poisoned cup. He wasn't there.

"Where are Merlin's personal chambers?" I asked Houdain. "Maybe he turned in early?"

"You're very close." Mordred's voice echoed down the hall as he strolled toward us.

Chapter 9
ANNA

I froze.

It was like watching a ferocious bear walk directly toward me, but my feet wouldn't move.

In fact, none of us were moving. Khalid at least had the frame of mind to shift his body into a defensive stance, but his feet were rooted too.

Were we being spelled and didn't know it?

Or were we all intimidated by the approaching Mordred?

As Mordred stopped in front of us, his dark eyes swept over our little group. He smiled. "How lovely. My accusers in the flesh. Very brave for two little girls."

I flinched. His tone was demeaning on purpose, yet none of us responded. I had thought for sure Bronwyn would take the bait, but for once she chose caution over rash anger.

We didn't know how powerful he was; his skills could've been far superior to ours, and agitating the man didn't seem like a good idea.

I finally built up enough courage to speak. "We'll be leaving to our chambers now, thank you very much."

I tried to walk away.

Frozen.

We *were* spelled!

Frantically, I swung my head around to view the others, and they were all desperately trying to move their feet.

Mordred had rooted us in place with magic.

My heart raced. The evil son of King Arthur was going to kill us all where we stood, or torture us, or . . .

"Why are you doing this?" I asked, trying to keep the terror from my voice.

Out of the corner of my eye, I could see both Bronwyn and Houdain staring straight ahead, hands clenched, trying to concentrate. They were probably attempting to break out of the spell. I figured my best bet was to keep Mordred busy while they worked on freeing us.

Mordred stepped closer to me and placed a finger under my chin. "Such a beauty." Then he laughed. "And such thoughts!"

I rounded my eyes at him. Thoughts? Was Mordred reading my mind? That was far worse than being trapped! I had no idea how to push someone out of my head. I had heard of astral projection spells and telepathy spells, but they were too advanced for me, and I had never had any interest in that type of magic.

I was reconsidering that stance right about now.

I desperately wanted to block him out before he saw anything embarrassing.

"In love with Khalid, are we?" Mordred snickered.

Like that.

I couldn't bear to face Khalid. He already knew how I felt, but to have Mordred read my mind and say it again was humiliating.

Mordred's finger left my chin, and he shook his head. "So tragic."

Tragic? My stomach turned. It was because Khalid didn't like me like that. I knew it with every fiber of my soul. Mordred had entered all of our minds, and Khalid probably viewed me as a pathetic, annoying girl who should leave him alone. He was there to protect and guard Bronwyn and me, and my silly feelings made him uncomfortable.

Before Mordred could confirm Khalid's indifference toward me, I said, "You've magically trapped us here to humiliate us? What a winner."

Mordred's expression turned angry and dark. "I'm humiliating you in private; you two had no such manners. What did you think would happen when you told the entire court and my father that I was trying to poison him? Did you think I would let that go without punishment?"

Punishment?

We were in serious trouble.

Mordred softened a bit, then eyed Khalid. "And no, it's not *tragic* because he thinks nothing of you. It's tragic because he's in love with you."

My heart nearly stopped.

Khalid?

In love with *me*?

I didn't want to believe for fear that Mordred was lying. I would be devastated if I allowed myself to truly fall in love with Khalid only to find that Khalid felt nothing for me.

"And that's tragic because . . . ?" I prodded. I still couldn't look at Khalid.

Bronwyn and Houdain had nothing to say about the matter; their eyes were now squeezed shut, and they were concentrating even harder.

It was just me and Mordred.

Mordred smiled wickedly. "You don't know, do you?"

He knew I didn't. I still couldn't tell if he was lying or not. After all, there were four of us frozen in the middle of hallway because this jerk had spelled us there. Lying would've been pretty low on the list of sins for Mordred at this point.

"You know I don't," I replied.

"Avalon guards take a vow of blood before they're allowed on the island. Tell me, dear Anna, did you ever find it odd that not one guard and not one priestess ever coupled?" Mordred spoke to me as if I were an idiot child.

And perhaps I was. When thinking about it, I had never seen a guard and priestess together. I knew a ton of girls who had crushes on guards, but nothing ever came of it.

Apparently, Mordred saw me coming to this conclusion because he laughed again. "Poor thing. You thought you could have a future with little Khalid here, didn't you?"

Khalid grunted.

I finally glanced at Khalid. His face was in a snarl of rage. I had never seen him this angry before. If he hadn't been frozen, I would have been scared for Mordred. At this point, though, I wished Merlin would walk in and crack a lightning bolt on Mordred's noggin.

Mordred's face lit up at Khalid's anger. "That's right, Priestess Anna. Khalid's blood vow is contingent on his life in Avalon. If he were ever to be caught laying hands on a priestess in an inappropriate way"—he cupped his hands as if telling me a secret—"that includes kissing, mind you"—he took his hands down and grinned—"Khalid would be banished from Avalon forever."

My heart sank, and a lump formed in my throat. I wanted to scream. I wanted to . . . I didn't even know. If I hadn't been spelled into place, I would have been frozen in misery. Sure, it was a fantasy, but in the back of my head, I'd always held hope that maybe someday I could be with Khalid. Now it was all gone.

My chest ached with sadness.

"So," Mordred said, "the only way you two lovebirds could ever be together is if you leave the life of an Avalon priestess behind, as in no magic, no island, everything you've ever known: gone. All for a guard?" He nudged Khalid, who actually growled. "I wouldn't get my hopes up, boy. These priestesses are pretty greedy when it comes to their magic."

Boom!

Mordred's eyes opened slightly as Bronwyn (bless her!) shattered the spell that bound her. The rest of us were still locked in place, but at least she was free.

Without hesitation, Bronwyn grabbed Mordred's forearms and screamed.

Mordred's skin turned as bright red as mine had when Bronwyn's magic had burned me.

Mordred grunted in pain, but his eyes showed a different story.

He *loved* the pain.

But more importantly, he seemed to love that *Bronwyn* was responsible for it, as if he had been waiting for her to break the spell and attack.

Swoosh!

Bronwyn's body flew back into my frozen body, and we

toppled to the ground.

Ouch.

She quickly gathered herself together, scrambling to launch back on Mordred, but he waved his hand, and Bronwyn froze once more.

On top of me.

Great.

"Very powerful." He grinned as he examined his reddened arms. "But so out of control." Mordred leaned down to Bronwyn's ear and spoke to her as if she were his lover. "I was like you once, but I learned to harness my magic. I could teach you."

Bronwyn spat on Mordred's face. "I'd rather die."

Mordred leaned back and shrugged. "That could be arranged, but I may have use for you two, so unfortunately, as fun as this whole meeting was, I'm going to have to erase it from your minds."

Bronwyn glared at Mordred with seething hatred. "If you think you can cast some spell and make us forget you're evil, you're delusional. We'll *never* forget. We'll *never* let you hurt King Arthur or anyone else."

"Brave words, but foolish ones. You, my dear Bronwyn, will be the easiest to make forget. Do you want to know why?" Mordred didn't wait for Bronwyn's potential verbal lashing. "Because you, more than the others, *want* to forget. All you've ever wanted to do is fit in, and now you're in Camelot, about to train with the mighty Merlin, and you've already accused the king's son of trying to murder him. Not exactly making yourself welcome, are you?"

Before Bronwyn could react, Mordred began incanting, then waved his hands in front of us.

"Get off of me!" I pushed Bronwyn away.

Bronwyn stumbled forward slightly as she used my hip as

purchase to stand. Her mouth dropped open, but she didn't speak.

Why were we on the floor?

She must have tripped and fallen on top of me. As I gathered myself to stand, Khalid reached down, helping me to my feet.

"I don't remember stopping here," Bronwyn said.

"Or using me to break your fall, it seems." I couldn't remember stopping either, but I didn't want to admit that for some reason.

Khalid moved ahead of us, his instincts on high alert.

Mine were too, but I had no idea why. It was a feeling I couldn't shake.

The four of us were alone in the hallway, and it felt as if we had been made of ice and someone finally thawed us.

"Do you think magic was used on us?" I asked Bronwyn.

Bronwyn began to nod, then paused, thinking. Slowly, she shook her head. "No. I don't think so. I think we're just tired."

Now that she'd said it, I *did* feel tired. Really tired. As in I could sleep for a thousand days tired.

"Yeah, you're right. It's late . . . isn't it?" My feet wobbled with unsteadiness, my thoughts disoriented. I didn't know what time of day it was.

I peered out a window as we headed toward the stairwell. It was indeed nighttime.

Houdain finally spoke. He sounded a little dazed himself. "Did I show you everything you wanted to see?"

That's right. Houdain had taken us on a tour of Camelot. I was embarrassed because I couldn't remember a single place he'd shown us. I really was tired. I didn't want to be impolite, so I lied. "Oh yes, you were a wonderful guide. Thank you, Houdain."

"Yes, thank you, Houdain," Bronwyn echoed. From the expression on her face, I could tell the tour hadn't been memorable to her either.

After we'd traveled up the stairs and arrived at our room, Houdain bid us good night and left.

Khalid led us into the room and then exited, closing the door behind him. He seemed more on edge than usual, so he'd probably stand guard all night. I couldn't blame him. I sensed it too.

I simply couldn't place why.

"Well, good night, Bronwyn," I said with very little attitude. I was too tired to argue or even be irritated by her.

She must have felt the same way because she answered back, "Good night, Anna."

We crawled into our large bed, each taking a side without argument.

Closing my eyes, I fell asleep instantly.

***

"Lady Anna, breakfast is being served." The voice of my housemaid, Gretchen, sang out to me.

I opened my eyes, and I was in my parent's home.

Definitely a dream.

I loved dreams where I was conscious. I didn't have them often, but when I did, I tried to remember every moment to relive when I awoke. Sometimes I was conscious enough I could actually control what happened. Those were a true treat.

In this one, I appeared to be a passenger only.

I sat down at the kitchen table, where my mother, father, and brother were already seated. My brother appeared to be five years old, which was the age he'd been when I left for Avalon. It was the last time I had seen him. He'd be about fifteen by now, so I had no idea what he looked like. It made my heart squeeze with homesickness. I received letters from family every week in Avalon, so I was well aware of how their lives were faring, but it wasn't the same as seeing them in person.

Being a noble family, we had a bigger house than most, but not as big as a keep or fortress. I remembered this room well. Father called it our breakfast den. It was off the kitchen and not as formal as our dining room. It had a small circular oak table, which was surrounded by pine benches. Morning light poured in through the large windows on the south-facing wall, and I could barely see the tops of the nearby pines in the distant forest. One tapestry of Father's coat of arms hung from the west wall, and on the east wall was a painting of his mother and father. A swinging wooden door that led to the kitchen was behind me.

My mother ate quietly at the table, as did my brother and father.

Why was I dreaming about them? I wasn't sure if I should say something.

Gretchen, a young woman in her twenties, though she'd be in her thirties by now, served me a hard-boiled egg on a pewter egg stand and a cup of barley tea in Mother's finest porcelain. "Morning, Lady Anna."

"Good morning, Gretchen," I answered back.

I'd always liked Gretchen. She used to play with me when her duties were finished for the day.

My family, meanwhile, said nothing. They simply ate and drank in silence, acting as if I weren't there.

Gretchen didn't leave back to the kitchen like she used to; instead, she sat down next to me. If this had been real life, my mother would have fainted from the action.

Gretchen stared at me, and I waited for her to say something. I shifted uncomfortably as her eyes remained on mine.

"What is it, Gretchen?" I asked, hoping for the dream to move in another direction.

Gretchen's eyes widened, and then she screamed, "The king will die!"

***

I awoke with a start.

What was that about?

My gifts weren't of a psychic nature, so I was pretty sure the dream wasn't prophetic, but it made my heart race all the same.

Bronwyn was already awake and brushing her hair at the vanity. "Bad dream?" She sounded almost . . . concerned.

I nodded. "Nonsense, really. I dreamt that my serving maid from back home told me that the king would die."

Bronwyn shrugged. "Weird."

That was it?

But what had I expected? The dream *was* weird. Had I really thought Bronwyn would read anything else into it?

Yes. For some reason, I had thought that.

I shook my head clear of my crazy thoughts. "We start training with Merlin today." The excitement that burned inside me caused my stomach to churn.

Bronwyn's eyes lit up. "Shall we?"

I dressed quickly and combed my hair, and then we were off.

Houdain met us at our door as if he had slept outside of it all night.

Khalid seemed to materialize out of nowhere and followed us as we made our way to Merlin's chambers.

I secretly peered over my shoulder at Khalid to get a quick peek at his beauty. When our eyes met, an immense sadness threated to knock me off my feet.

It was so strange I immediately turned away.

What had that been about?

He'll never like me the way I like him. That's why I'm feeling so sad. Today is the day I finally realized it.

I tried not to let the feelings of dejection overtake me. We were going to train with *Merlin*. I didn't want to ruin that with my insecurities.

Arriving at Merlin's study was like a dream come true. Though we had seen glimpses of the room through Priestess Elaine's mirror on Avalon, in person it was more impressive. There were shelves lined with books both ancient and newly bound, bottles of every shape imaginable filled with liquids, herbs, and substances—most of which I didn't even recognize—and knickknacks that I was positive weren't actually knickknacks at all.

Is that a dragon claw?

The stone walls were barely visible through not only his stacked shelves but the other clutter propped up against them: robes hanging on metal hooks, gnarled wood walking sticks, a few cauldrons of varying sizes, a rickety ladder I would be too frightened to use, and end tables covered with more dried herbs and bottles. Even the wooden ceiling beams were difficult to see with a hanging candelabrum filled with candles and drying herbs blowing slightly in the wind from the four high windows above.

The only clear space in the entire room was a large wooden table that stood waist high with no chairs or benches surrounding it.

Merlin waved us to the table, and my heart jumped into my throat. This was it. We were finally going to learn.

"After talking with Houdain last evening, I've decided to begin your training learning the art of telepathy," Merlin announced.

106

Telepathy? I had been expecting potions or herb lore. Invading the mind wasn't on my list of things I wanted to do.

"That's so invasive," Bronwyn said. To my surprise, we were on the exact same page.

"Yes, Master Merlin," I said. "Maybe we should start with something more suited for us?" I suggested, not knowing why.

Just the idea of telepathy gave me goose bumps.

"Why do you think that, Priestess Anna?" he asked with a slight bend of his head.

I opened my mouth to answer, but nothing came out. Finally, I confessed, "I honestly don't know. I just don't like the sound of it."

"I feel the same, Master Merlin," Bronwyn admitted. Again with the surprise.

"I'd normally move on since I've been told by Priestesses Florette and Elaine you two rarely agree, but in this instance, I'm disregarding your request. It sounds to me as if you are both frightened to learn telepathy, and fear is a good way to grow." He motioned toward Bronwyn. "Since this is soulbound work, we'll start with you."

My face flushed in embarrassment.

Rub it in, Master Merlin.

With a haughty smile, Bronwyn nodded to Merlin. "What should I do?"

"I want you to concentrate on Anna. Try to envision her thoughts, her feelings, her memories." He turned to me. "And I want you to think of one word and repeat it over and over in your head."

That was easy.

Annoying, annoying, annoying.

107

Bronwyn stared me down, concentrating.

Tap. Tap. Tap.

I shuddered.

"Master Merlin," I said, "I feel a wall in my mind as if it's made of stone."

"Sh, I'm trying to concentrate," Bronwyn said.

"No, no, Bronwyn, I need you two to tell me everything that feels odd." His eyes pierced mine. "Anna, can you break this wall? Is it of your own doing?"

"Why wouldn't it be of my own doing? Are you saying Bronwyn put a wall in my head?" I exclaimed. That had to be it! It was just like Bronwyn to try to control me.

"I did not!" Bronwyn huffed. "I wouldn't even know how, and the last place I would ever want to be is in *your* head." She let out a frustrated sigh. "Annoying."

"Hey! That's my word!" I said with a smile.

Bronwyn grinned widely.

My mind suddenly went blank.

What were we talking about again?

Had Master Merlin taught us something? I couldn't seem to remember the last few minutes.

"Are we going to learn potions now?" I asked excitedly as Bronwyn nodded eagerly. It was nice that we were getting along so well. Who knew training with Merlin would bring us together like this?

Master Merlin stared at the two of us for a few more moments, his eyebrows crinkled and his lips pressed together. Sighing deeply, he nodded. "Let's move on then."

Move on? Move on from what?

When I glanced over at Bronwyn, her eyes mirrored the same

confusion, but neither of us said a word.

Merlin didn't elaborate, so I figured he'd misspoken, and I was thrilled when he heeded my request and started us with potions. Bronwyn was a little frustrated, potions not really being her forte, but she mixed a few better than I did. (I would never admit that to her though!)

We moved on to telepathy, which felt strangely familiar, almost as if we had already tried it before. Neither Bronwyn nor I liked telepathy, though, and we complained to each other each night since he made us practice it for the next few weeks. We both admitted to feeling strangely invaded by the whole thing. Merlin made a point to have us study the subject more than any of the others, which only agitated us further. On this, Bronwyn and I agreed wholeheartedly.

Telekinesis, on the other hand, we both excelled at. Well, Bronwyn definitely had me beat; she'd levitated an entire table (without destroying it, which was a miracle!). I'd levitated a single piece of parchment, but I'd done it without using an incantation, so I was happy.

Life at Camelot was becoming comfortable. I didn't get to spend much time with Khalid, but what had I expected? He was our guard, not my suitor, no matter how much I wished it were otherwise. Besides, I couldn't shake the sadness that crept inside of me every time I saw him. It grew stronger every day, and I could tell he sensed it too. I didn't know what to do about it, so I chose to ignore it.

We met all sorts of people at dinner every night, though some of them gave us strange looks the first couple of nights, as if we had done something unforgiveable. But strangely, the friendlier the king's son, Mordred, was to us in public, the kinder everyone acted.

We sat at the high table with Merlin and the king and sometimes his knights. Sir Gawain and Sir Lancelot were the most amiable, always with a quick quip or jest to liven the mood, but Sir Galahad had the best stories.

Mordred was the most fascinating. He always asked me and Bronwyn a ton of questions about how our life was back in Avalon. Arthur seemed surprised that Bronwyn and I got along so well with his son, but he appeared happy nonetheless.

My dreams of Gretchen had happened every night since the first one, but every night she'd say something new. Last night's had been the weirdest because she sang at me, saying, "Time, time, time, you're wasting time."

I dressed in my nightgown and lay in bed wondering what new thing Gretchen had to say to me tonight.

Closing my eyes, I was about to find out.

***

I was so used to this dream by now that I didn't wait for Gretchen to call me to breakfast. I simply walked to the table and sat down, completely ignoring my family.

Gretchen served me the egg and tea, then sat down.

I made faces at her while she did her usual staring contest.

Her mouth opened.

Here it comes.

What new piece of insanity was she about to tell me?

"The vow. Anna, Khalid has taken a vow."

What?

For a moment, I froze.

What?

My stomach twisted so intensely I couldn't breathe, though it was only a dream.

What?

***

"Anna! Anna!" I awoke fighting for breath.

Bronwyn stood over me, patting my back as if I had been choking.

"You weren't breathing! You were gasping for air!" Bronwyn yelled, eyes wide and frantic.

Gretchen's words rang in my ears so loudly I wanted to scream. *The vow. Anna, Khalid has taken a vow.*

Then, like a dam breaking, everything rushed back into my brain. All my memories were restored instantly: Mordred freezing us, telling us horrible things, planning the death of his father, and erasing all of our memories of him.

My mind had been trying to break his spell this entire time. Gretchen, someone I trusted from home, had been giving me clues every night. But it was the reminder that Khalid and I could never be together that had finally broken the enchantment.

Bronwyn waited for me to speak. How was I going to get through to her when it had taken me so long to get through to myself?

"I'm fine, Bronwyn, thank you. I must have . . . swallowed a fly or something," I said.

Bronwyn's face relaxed.

Okay. Here goes.

"Bronwyn?"

"Yes?" Her head tilted to the side quizzically.

"You're under a spell."

111

Chapter 10
BRONWYN

I was not under a spell. I felt fine. I must have had a strange expression on my face, though, because Anna said, "I'm telling you, my dreams have been warning me this whole time, trying to snap me out of Mordred's spell." She took a deep breath. "Remember when we saw him in the hallway a few weeks ago? The night before we began training with Merlin? After Mordred had tried to poison Arthur?"

"What are you talking about?"

"Do you remember arriving at Camelot?" she asked slowly, as if I were too stupid to understand.

"Of course I do! Are you suggesting that someone made me forget something?"

"Isn't that obvious by my line of questioning, Bronwyn?" Anna sighed in frustration.

I seriously didn't know why she thought I had been spelled to forget anything.

"We came to Camelot. Houdain met us first, then the king and queen, and Merlin, of course. Houdain showed us around. We had dinner. We started training. Those dreams must have been super bad, but they were *just* dreams."

"No, they weren't," she insisted, starting to pace. "This last dream broke the spell. I woke up and remembered everything." The look on her face was . . . priceless, honestly. She'd had multiple nightmares, and the one that had made her choke suddenly convinced her we were under a forgetting spell? The longer this went on, the less funny it was to see that angry, frustrated expression on her face. "Tell me *exactly* what happened at the first dinner."

"We ate too much," I said. "Houdain kept asking me if I liked the food and said he'd bring me more if I wanted it."

"Okay. Before that. What happened right before we entered the dining hall?"

I thought about it, trying to remember every little detail. "Houdain was showing us around, and we saw Mordred."

"Right. What happened next?"

"He was walking ahead of us down a hallway. He stopped and turned around, and then he introduced himself."

Anna shook her head.

"I can go on," I said. "He was wearing dark clothes."

"No," she said. "You already got it wrong."

"What do you mean? What exactly am I missing?"

"We followed Mordred to Merlin's potion room, and—"

"No we didn't," I said.

"We did," she insisted. She scrunched up her face at me, annoyed. "Let's get to Merlin already."

***

". . . and the moment I woke up, I remembered everything that had happened." Anna told her story to Merlin with a flourish. Her hands and arms were flying everywhere, emphasizing every emotional expression. "But she doesn't believe me," she continued, pointing at me.

"I say she's been having vivid dreams and this one finally broke her," I said.

Merlin merely glanced at me. To Anna, he said in his deep, slightly rough voice, "Let us have a chat." He signaled for me to stay as he walked with Anna to the door of his chambers and left with her.

I was alone.

Obviously, I wasn't invited, but they didn't go far because I wasn't yanked against the closed door. Why would he tell Anna something and not me? Something I wasn't ready for? Oh, great. If that was the case, Anna would gloat about her superiority *forever*!

I put my ear against the wood but heard nothing.

I had to know what they were saying. I hated this position. People had talked about me all the time in my village, but it hadn't bothered me unless I'd known they were doing it, like whispering and glancing in my direction. I didn't know why that made a difference. Out of sight, out of mind? I might not have been able to see Anna, but I knew she was getting information that I should know too. I didn't want to leave it up to her to decide when I should know something.

Could I spell myself to enhance my hearing? Upon considering it, the idea felt very doable. This was odd because normally when I thought about performing magic, I panicked. That whole out-of-control-burning-forests-emptying-lakes thing. I took it as a good omen and closed my eyes. I concentrated as hard as I could, thinking about my ears and hearing things loudly. I cupped my hands over my ears to emphasize where I wanted the spell to hit me. Merlin had tried to teach me to visualize my powers as a glowing white ball that traveled through me, so I pictured the white ball moving into my ears.

So many sounds!

Tons of people talking.

Horses neighing and clomping about.

Dogs barking.

Metalwork.

Music.

Swords!

I pushed one ear hard against the door and covered the other ear with a hand, hoping this would block out everything except my target. After a few moments, my hearing focused.

"That's good. Your sleeping mind was telling you something was wrong, and it finally connected to your waking mind," Merlin said. "And as a result of this experience, you have mastered your first task."

There was a long pause, and then Anna said, "Telepathy. Because the spell came from Mordred's mind, I broke that connection."

"Very good," Merlin said.

"But I can hardly use it. There's so much to learn."

"Indeed. But what you must keep present in your thoughts is that you accomplished a raw magic that did not require an incantation."

There was no conversation for a moment. I imagined Anna feeling proud of herself. Telepathy was difficult. I was still long from getting it right, and I had that raw magic ability already.

"What about Bronwyn?" Anna asked. I'd known I'd enter the conversation at some point. Was she going to rub it in?

"You must use your new gift to help her."

"But I'm not—"

"It is your next task."

There were a few things racing around my mind at that moment. First, Anna had accomplished a task that I had not yet. Second, I would have to take Anna's help to remember whatever it was that I'd forgotten. Third, I really was under a memory-wiping spell!

And Mordred had cast it.

But he was such a nice person!

And kind of handsome in an older man sort of way.

I found it very hard to believe that Mordred would ever try to hurt anything, except maybe someone he was battling against.

"What about Mordred, Master?" she asked.

"That we will discuss when Bronwyn can participate in the conversation." The way he said that made me stand straight up and step away from the door. Intensely, I focused on my ears, breaking the hearing spell right as the door opened and they returned to the room.

Merlin pulled out a stool and indicated for me to sit. He held out his hand as if presenting me to Anna.

Anna breathed in deep, gathering her confidence.

"What's going on?" I asked.

"I'm going to break the spell you're under," she said. "Why aren't you surprised, Bronwyn?"

I looked at Merlin, my face burning.

He *knew* I had listened to their private conversation, but from the slight lifting of his chin, he seemed proud of me in spite of his nonreactionary face.

I sighed. "I cast a spell on myself to enhance my hearing to listen to you and Master Merlin."

"What?" Anna fumed. "That's rude! Disrespectful! How could you, Bronwyn?" She turned toward Merlin. His relaxed face seemed to make her angrier. "This is unacceptable behavior for a priestess of Avalon, Master!"

"What Bronwyn chooses to do with her powers is her privilege and responsibility, Anna. Indeed, she successfully cast a specific spell to accomplish a task, which was to gather information."

"It's eavesdropping," she said.

"Which is what she did several weeks ago, allowing her to overhear Mordred's plans to kill Arthur."

"I did?"

Merlin nodded.

Huh. Well, at the moment, I focused on the fact that Merlin had said I accomplished a task *and* that I'd successfully completed a spell without it going crazy and destroying things.

I grinned.

Anna's shoulders fell, and she sighed as she turned back toward me. "Hold still, Bronwyn."

I did. I sat there staring at Anna, whose eyes were squeezed closed.

Since nothing was happening, I glanced across the room at Merlin, who was cleaning his fingernails with the tip of a long, narrow knife. He wasn't paying attention at all.

Or he was but hid it well.

I couldn't believe he knew I had been listening to his conversation with Anna. But then I did believe it because, well, he was Merlin. He was the most powerful magic user ever known by Avalon, which had already existed for thousands of years. So that was saying a lot. If he lived backward, as some said, he would know everything that would happen. No one said he looked younger the longer they'd known him though. Every description I had ever heard of him stated that he appeared old and his eyes looked ancient. That was exactly the man who sat across the room from me now—

Bam!

My vision dipped to black.

Whoosh!

I blinked rapidly as the room and everything in it became vivid and bright.

I fell backward off the stool.

"Bronwyn!" Anna yelled. She helped me up before I could reorient myself. "Do you remember?"

"Remember what?" I asked. I didn't know what she wanted from me.

"Bronwyn! Just . . . tell me everything you remember from the last few weeks."

"Oh. You mean that Mordred is trying to kill the king and that he cast—oh, wow!" It all flooded back in a wave: the spell being cast, the sensation of losing memories, not having certain memories and then having all those memories again. It was like living two lives at once. That was one powerful spell. "What do we do now?"

"Nothing," Merlin said, still cleaning his fingernails.

"As priestesses of Avalon, it's our duty to protect the king," Anna insisted.

"You are incorrect," Merlin said. "As priestesses who are still training and are guests of mine, your duty is to study."

"We can't do nothing, Master," I said, finally regaining some composure.

"You can study," he said. "You need your powers sharpened and ready."

Ready?

I gulped.

"Ready for what?" Anna's voice squeaked.

Merlin brushed the question aside and said, "You should never put yourself in harm's way. From now on, what Mordred does is only your concern if it directly affects you. Everything else is my business alone."

Merlin was right. Mordred was clearly much more powerful than we were and definitely very dangerous. He'd had all four of us completely frozen. And even after I'd managed to pull myself free, he had the power to do it again. We needed to train if we were ever to face him again as enemies.

"I've had a lot of time to think on this." Merlin placed the knife down, his eyes now trained on ours. "When I realized the two of you had no recollection of confronting Mordred and Arthur in a room full of people, I knew Mordred had cast a memory spell on you. Breaking that spell became your first lesson."

Anna nodded. "That's why you kept making us practice telepathy."

"Which we completely failed," I grumbled.

"It took time, yes, but Anna accomplished the task. Your mind has been practicing the art of telepathy for weeks now, and that allowed Anna to break through to you." Merlin sat a little taller on his stool, nodding at us with a hint of approval.

"But if you knew our memories had been wiped and that Mordred was trying to kill the king, why didn't you do anything about it?" I said before I could stop myself. *Good one, Bronwyn. Accuse the most powerful magician of all time of being a coward.*

But Merlin didn't appear at all fazed by my question. He simply tilted his head to the side as if dealing with a student who didn't quite understand the assignment. "Once I heard about this attempt, I started keeping a closer eye on both Mordred *and* King Arthur. But Mordred is no fool. He chose a memory-wiping spell over killing two priestesses of Avalon. He's smart enough to know what the island might do to him if you were harmed by his hand."

"You mean what Priestesses Elaine and Florette might do to him?"

"No. I did not mean that," Merlin answered cryptically.

"I knew it!" Anna exclaimed triumphantly.

"Knew what?" I asked, slightly annoyed with her exuberance.

"That Avalon is alive. I could feel it. I often thought I was just imagining it because I desperately needed a friend." She gave me a pointed look, then refocused on Merlin. "Can the island . . . attack Mordred? From *here*?"

Merlin raised his eyebrows. "I've seen Avalon do a number of incredible acts of magic over the years, and let's just say that I wouldn't want to cross her."

Whoa. Avalon was *alive*. And she had our backs. My heart surged with an even deeper love for the island I'd called home for the last few years. My head swam with questions, but from Merlin's vague answer, I knew I'd get nothing more from him.

It wasn't important though. What was important was protecting King Arthur.

"Was this the first time Mordred tried to kill his father?" I asked instead. Had Merlin been secretly battling against the king's son for years? If that *had* been the first attempt, what would have happened had Anna and I not been there? Would Arthur have been dead right now?

Merlin was calm about everything. I wondered if that was how he always reacted. Maybe he'd been around long enough to not be surprised by anything anymore.

"It was not the first attempt, and you girls did indeed save Arthur, which I am indebted to you for. You two calling Mordred out so publicly has made him lurk in the shadows, which is a very good thing. He hasn't tried anything since then."

Merlin let that sit with us for a few moments, and then he stood. "Today's lessons are over. Priestesses, I suggest searching for my apprentice and your guardian to repair their memories. You should try, Bronwyn. For practice."

I wasn't quite finished with my questions. "Master, what do we do if we find out about something else Mordred has planned?"

"Tell me."

"What if there's no time?"

"Priestess, if you interfere again and blame Mordred without proof, Arthur will force my hand and send you back to Avalon."

I nodded in understanding. We left quietly, closing the door behind us. Khalid would be nearby.

Khalid.

I remembered what Mordred had said about Khalid and the look that had been on Anna's face. It was simply heartbreaking. "Anna," I said quietly. "I'm sorry."

"It's okay," she said. "I guess we shouldn't try to hide things from each other anyway."

She thought I was apologizing for using the hearing spell.

"I meant about Khalid."

Her face darkened—not in anger, but in anguish. My insides churned in guilt about bringing it up, but I wanted to let her know I understood.

"Mordred is pure evil," she said.

"If there's a way that you and Khalid can be together, we'll find it," I said, right before he let his presence be known.

Anna wouldn't make eye contact with him, and his furrowed brows gave away his concern.

He currently had no idea she knew the truth about how he felt and the tragedy of their feelings for each other. That would change soon. My chest squeezed for both of them.

"Let's find Houdain," she said.

I let the subject drop. "Hey, wait," I said. I leaned in close enough to whisper, "I think we should pretend around Mordred that we're still under his spell."

Anna nodded. "I completely agree. He thinks we're all friends. Let's keep it that way." Taking a shaky breath, she added, "If he found out we were lying . . ."

"We're under Merlin's protection and apparently the protection of Avalon herself," I said, not able to hide the awe in my voice.

Anna's entire face lit up. "Right? We'll have to ask Priestesses Florette and Elaine more about that." Then she bit her lower lip in thought. "By pretending we're still under his spell, we might be able to find out more about him. He probably wouldn't ever share any real secrets with us though."

"No, but as long as he thinks we trust him completely, he might let his guard drop at least a little."

"Agreed," Anna said, and we started walking to find Houdain. "But I think we also need to keep an eye out for King Arthur ourselves," she said in a more normal speaking voice. "I know Merlin said he's watching Mordred, but he missed the poisoning completely, and Mordred might try something again long before we gain any of his trust."

Not a truer word had been spoken.

We found Houdain walking toward us, carrying some colored cloth. He grinned broadly as we approached. "Finished for the day, priestesses?"

"We need you to come with us," I said quietly. "You're under a spell."

Houdain's eyebrows went up. "I am? When did this happen?"

I was sure Anna felt as if she were reliving the same moment, except I didn't think Houdain would be as argumentative as I'd been.

"You too, Khalid," Anna said.

Merlin had told us to study and leave all the heroics to him, but we never promised to avoid the king. So hopefully, as long as Mordred thought we were innocently hanging out around Arthur, he would not consider us a threat.

Chapter 11
ANNA

Working together, we removed Mordred's spell from Houdain and Khalid rather quickly. Once I had figured out how to do it on Bronwyn, having the extra help made it easier, which was nice. Mordred must've thought we were complete and utter fools. And he wasn't wrong. I wondered how we'd be able to pretend that we were still under his spell next time we encountered him. I wasn't very good at hiding things from people, and I didn't trust that Bronwyn would be very good at it either. Then again, she'd hid her powers for years, supposedly, so maybe she could be the one to have direct contact with Mordred. I could avoid eye contact and lag behind.

I replayed all the conversations I'd had with Mordred while under his spell. My ears burned thinking about some of them. The way he'd laughed with us, now I realized he'd been laughing *at* us. I hated being perceived as stupid. My stomach twisted into knots. I shook the memories from my brain before I withered from embarrassment. It would be difficult not to scowl at him every time he smiled at us.

Khalid's eyes met mine, and he asked gently, "May I speak to you in private, Priestess Anna?"

My limbs, my face, my brain—nothing could move. Finally, I managed to break free, but all I could do was nod.

What if Mordred had been lying? I knew in my gut that the blood oath was real because Mordred was right: I had no recollection of any priestess being with an Avalon guard. What I couldn't accept as being real was Khalid being in love with me. My face burned from embarrassment knowing that I loved him. I barely knew him, though I'd spent hours watching him on Avalon and felt as if I knew him intimately. But I was a naïve little girl who had a crush, wasn't I?

I followed Khalid to the window of our room. Bronwyn and Houdain politely excused themselves and stood just outside the doorway. It was about as far as our tether would allow us to be apart from each other. I appreciated the privacy though. I didn't feel like being humiliated in front of Bronwyn *and* Houdain.

When we reached the window, Khalid's eyes met mine. "We should talk."

The brown in his eyes had little flecks of black that took my breath away. He stared at me with such intensity that my knees started to buckle. I caught myself before I mortified myself further.

"Okay. Talk," I said way more abruptly than I'd intended, but I needed him to speak first because I was too terrified to admit how deep my feelings were for him only to find out I was right and he didn't see me in that way.

Khalid didn't skip a beat, apparently used to my abruptness. "Mordred was right."

I needed to know the facts before I could process what was happening. It was the scholar in me. I suddenly found the courage to clarify. "About the vow, or about how you feel about me?"

Khalid's forehead creased in concern, which almost certainly meant he didn't want to hurt my feelings.

Then he said, "Both."

"Both," I repeated.

I stared at him in disbelief. I couldn't seem to comprehend what he was telling me.

His eyes were downcast, sad. "I see that he lied about how you feel about me."

My heart ached at hearing those words. His shoulders slumped as if he was defeated and heartbroken.

Before I could think through my answer, I blurted, "I love you."

Oh. My. Goddess.

Bronwyn would've laughed at me if she had heard, and knowing her, she was probably listening in at the door.

But Khalid's face lit up, and I suddenly didn't care if anyone overheard me. He cupped my cheeks with his hands, and his eyes sparkled as he stared into mine. His perfectly full lips edged up into a smile that made him the most beautiful human being I had ever seen. Did he truly love me too?

But that was impossible.

Utterly impossible.

He didn't even know me.

He'd barely talked to me in Avalon.

Khalid must have seen the doubt in my eyes because he quickly said, "I love you, Anna."

It was the first time he hadn't called me Priestess Anna, just

Anna, and it made me shiver in excitement. I had never wanted someone to kiss me more.

"But how?" I asked instead. "How could you love me? You don't know me." I voiced my worst fears and pulled his hands away from my face. "It certainly couldn't be because you find me attractive. I'm not beautiful at all—not like Bronwyn, not like Joanna. You must be under a spell. Mordred must have cast a spell on you to torture me!" That was it. It had to be it. I couldn't see any other explanation. It was obvious why *I* liked Khalid, but why would he like *me*? Before Mordred had set the forgetting spell, he had set a love spell. To be mean. I wanted to tear him to pieces!

"I'm not under a spell, Anna."

There he went, calling me by my given name. My senses couldn't take it. I was about to pass out. Maybe *I* was under a spell.

Khalid said, "You would have seen it when you removed the forgetting spell, correct?" He was using my deduction skills on me. And what he said made sense. I would have been able to see another spell if there had been one.

But that would mean . . .

He *did* love me.

My doubts overrode me again. "But he's a powerful magician. I didn't know what I was looking for. I . . . You wouldn't even know you were under a spell. You'd think all your feelings were real, so I can't really believe what you say."

"Then go inside my head. Search wherever you want to. I trust you, Anna." He took my hands in his, and my goddess! The boy could make every nerve ending in my body tingle. I was a mess.

But I nodded. "I'm going to connect us through telepathy like I did before, and I'm going to check myself too. I have to know if I'm under a spell as well. Because right now . . ." I paused, not

127

sure if I should be completely honest with how I felt in case I *was* under a spell, but I decided since Khalid was being truthful, then so would I. "Right now, you're all I think about."

His hands squeezed tighter around mine, and my heart thudded against my ribs. If this was true love and not a spell, then I didn't know how I was going to function properly on a daily basis, especially if we could never be together. The thought of our lips never touching—not even once—left me feeling ripped in half.

Taking a deep breath, I stared into Khalid's hopeful eyes (that alone almost killed me!) and said, "Are you ready?"

Squeezing my hands once more, he answered simply, "Yes."

I closed my eyes, trying to ignore the constant shivers I had from being this close to him. The heat from his body radiated next to me. I wanted him to lift me into his arms and—

Stop!

Focus!

If this was a spell, it was a good one.

I needed to have full concentration if I was truly going to find out for sure if Mordred had spelled us, and concentration was really difficult when I could literally feel Khalid's soft breath on my forehead. He smelled of mint and lavender—

Stop!

Pushing all my senses aside, I imagined seeing inside Khalid's head, just as Bronwyn and I had done to remove the forgetting spell. But this time I was alone, which made the experience ten times more intimate. There wasn't anything substantive to see; it was more colors or auras. Magic—the forgetting spell—had floated around the inside of his head like a red cloud. Once the spell had been broken, there were no other colors that stood out. I concentrated harder to see if I had missed something before.

Another spell. A love spell. It was the only way to explain the intensity I felt for Khalid and vice versa.

But no matter how hard I searched, Khalid was clean of all spells.

There was nothing floating around, no colors out of the ordinary, nothing.

I reflected inward to see inside my own head.

Nothing either.

I opened my eyes and pulled my hands away from Khalid's gently.

I couldn't look at him. I had an overpowering fear that I couldn't explain. Now that I knew neither one of us was under any spell, my chest felt hollowed out. Even if Khalid had been only a fantasy to me, having it be real and then taken away before it had a chance to blossom was devastating.

Khalid's finger reached down and lifted my chin, so I was forced to make eye contact with him. His eyes were imploring, worried, and unsure all at once. "What did you find?" he asked.

I *found* that there were tears in my eyes. Why was I being so emotional? I barely knew Khalid! But that wasn't true. I *knew* him. I couldn't explain it. I couldn't rationalize it. But from the moment I'd laid eyes on him, I knew we were tied in some way. Our souls, our lives, were bound as strongly as Bronwyn and I were bound by magic. I'd denied it. I'd pretended it was a silly crush. I'd told myself over and over that someone like Khalid could never love me. But he could.

And gazing into his eyes, I knew he *did.*

I choked out the words, "We're not spelled."

Then his lips were on mine, and my entire body felt like exploding into a million pieces. I'd never been kissed before, and I now knew I only wanted to be kissed by Khalid for the rest of my life. His right hand cupped my face, holding it gently, as if I were a precious flower to him, while his other hand pulled me in closer. I could feel the desperation and desire as his lips pressed against mine, and it made me want him more.

I no longer had thoughts, just pure, raw emotion and an aching need to be closer to Khalid. No matter how close we were to each other, it didn't feel close enough. As both his hands now pulled me into him, his kisses moved from my mouth to my neck. Shivers ran through my entire being, and my eyes rolled back from the sensation.

I could no longer breathe. I could no longer think. I could no longer do anything but release my body and soul into Khalid. His kisses grew more and more intense. My mind went blissfully blank as I lost myself entirely to this moment.

"*Whoa!*" Bronwyn's voice cut through the air like a hammer to my brain.

We both jumped at her voice, acting like startled rabbits.

Bronwyn appeared utterly shocked but a little impressed as well, which was quite rude in my opinion. "I thought that was forbidden or something. Isn't that what Mordred said?"

Houdain simply stood there, shocked, his face white. It made me think the boy had never had any romantic experience in his life so far. To see it right in front of him obviously made him uncomfortable.

Speaking of which, my face still burned at having two people walk in on such an intimate moment. It only reminded me of the fact that since I was magically bound to Bronwyn, I'd never have privacy again.

I glanced quickly at Khalid, fearing I'd see regret in his eyes.

My heart sang with relief, as all I could see was the warmth of his gaze, his feelings for me radiating off of him like he was a fire in a hearth. I hoped he could see I felt exactly the same.

I finally answered Bronwyn's question. "It is forbidden, but we're not in Avalon. And Mordred said we'd have to be caught, so unless you plan on telling on us, this is a secret." My eyes searched hers, and I prayed she wouldn't have some moral obligation to tell Priestess Elaine or Florette. I didn't want to give up Khalid. Not now. Not when we'd finally connected.

Bronwyn shrugged. "Well, maybe if you get this"—she waved at us knowingly—"out of your system, you guys will be able to move on. You barely know each other, so maybe it's all chemistry."

That was insulting. It somehow cheapened what Khalid and I had, making it something physical and not the radiating love that pounded in my heart.

It was Khalid who spoke though, and he was angry. "Priestess Bronwyn, do not speak of what you don't understand. I have loved Anna from afar for the time I have been at Avalon. I may not have been able to express my feelings, but I *know* her better than anyone and certainly better than you. I may not say much, but I see everything that happens on the island. I watched as Anna rose above being ridiculed and beaten down by you and your followers. I watched as she found joy in the smallest of things, like a simple flower blooming amongst the cobblestones. I watched her save a robin's egg when it fell from its nest. I watched her find happiness in reading the many books from the library." He paused, emotional, then said very clearly, "I love Priestess Anna, and that will never change. I protect the both of you because I am bound by blood and would die for either one of you. And yes, by the laws of Avalon, I am forbidden to be with Anna and make her my wife. But know this: I would never ask Anna to leave Avalon, but I would break my blood vow if it meant I could have a life with her. And if it comes to that, I will."

Wife. He said *wife*! I'd marry him this instant if he asked.

But I couldn't. Not yet. Like he said, maybe someday. But I did make a promise to myself in that moment: I would never give Khalid up. Though my destiny was supposedly to govern Avalon someday, I would find a way to have both—*without* Khalid having to break his blood vow.

I waited for Bronwyn's snarky reply, but for the first time maybe ever, she shuffled her feet, a little bit embarrassed. "I wasn't trying to be mean to Anna. We simply get under each other's skin."

Khalid wasn't letting her off the hook, which made me love him more. "It doesn't change the fact that you let those girls isolate her until she had no friends. You ignored it because you were angry with her."

Bronwyn looked as if she had been slapped in the face, but she didn't deny it either. Then her eyes met mine, and her expression was one of regret. "I guess I didn't realize that. Or if I did, I didn't want to face it or acknowledge it. My village pushed me away and treated me as if I had a contagious disease. They thought I'd kill them with my magic. I know what it's like to be shunned and alone. I wouldn't wish that on anyone. If we didn't make each other so angry all the time, I might have seen that. I'm sorry."

Was that an actual apology?

I was too shocked to move.

But I answered, "I provoked you. A lot. I guess I was jealous of how the others worshipped you, and it hurt knowing how easy it was for them to hate me."

"I didn't want anyone to hate you." Bronwyn's voice was quiet, but she meant it.

Khalid's hand rested on my shoulder, and I reached up to hold it tightly.

Bronwyn took a deep breath, then said, "I promise I won't tell a soul about you two. And I'll give you your privacy if you ever need to . . . you know."

My face flushed. Surprisingly, Khalid wasn't ruffled at all, which wrenched my stomach in all sorts of ways. He simply nodded his thanks to Bronwyn.

Then all eyes were on Houdain.

Houdain swallowed hard, then nervously replied, "Me too. I won't tell anyone. Not even Master Merlin. I swear."

I relaxed into Khalid's body behind me. Knowing that we wouldn't be able to show our affection for each other in public, I wanted to feel him against me for as long as I could.

Bronwyn nodded toward the door. "If we're going to save the king from Mordred, we'd better get to following Arthur. We all good?"

I nodded, and so did Khalid.

Houdain appeared extremely relieved to be leaving the room. "He should be in the great hall about now. Let's get a move on."

Chapter 12
BRONWYN

As we walked back through the halls of Camelot on our way to find King Arthur in the great hall, Khalid's words repeated over and over in my head.

It doesn't change the fact that you let those girls isolate her until she had no friends.

I *had* done that.

Hearing Anna accuse me of the same thing, I'd dismissed it. It was easy when we were always at each other's throats. But Khalid had noticed. He had seen what I'd done and felt for Anna the way my family felt for me when our villagers had treated me the same.

Tears welled up in my eyes, and I blinked them away so no one would see. I wanted to apologize to her again, but I knew it wouldn't help. They were only words. I'd have to prove to Anna that I was sorry by my actions, not by my words. I didn't know how, but hopefully an opportunity would present itself in the coming days.

I peered over at Anna as we neared the great hall. I had

forgotten to be my true self on Avalon, and that had affected her directly.

"What?" she asked.

"Nothing."

Anna stopped walking and put her hands on her hips as she glared at me. She probably thought I was thinking something bad about her. We might not ever be friends, but she was starting to feel like a sister.

She eyed me suspiciously, then shrugged. "Okay, but if something's bothering you, we have to be honest with each other. No going off on your own."

"We're bound. I'm not doing anything by myself," I said snarkily. She just brought it out of me.

Houdain chimed in while we were stopped. "The great hall should be full this time of day from King Arthur holding court, so we can stay somewhat hidden in the crowd."

I breathed in deep. "You ready?"

"Goddess, I hope so," Anna said as she began walking again.

Keeping pace, we approached the great hall entrance and waited quietly until the guards opened the massive wooden doors for our small party of four.

Houdain had been right; the great hall *was* crowded. We inched closer to the back so we could gain a better view of the entire room and keep an eye on the king at the same time.

Searching for Mordred in the throng of people, we all came up with nothing.

I couldn't shake the familiar feeling of being out of my element despite having lived in Camelot for the last few weeks.

There were poor and rich alike in the hall. Anna had told me when we first arrived that most local kings never held court for anyone other than nobles or knights, but Arthur, who was the high king, would listen to peasants too. He heard their news and judged their problems as thoughtfully as he would those of any noble. I noticed some nobles sneered at the sight of the peasants, but they tried to hide their opinions when the king was looking.

Nobles parted for our small group. Our tan robes of Avalon kept people at a distance, though whether it was out of respect or fear of magic, I didn't know (probably a bit of both).

Finally reaching the back of the room, we situated ourselves, our eyes roaming the room for trouble.

There were only a few disputes left to settle, and as the king decided the final one, I couldn't shake the feeling that something was about to fall on my head. Instinctively, I glanced at the ceiling, but there were only windows and stonework, nothing that could drop on anyone.

I turned to Anna, but she was focused on Arthur. My eyes moved to Houdain, who stood inches behind me, scanning the hall.

I nudged Anna to tell her of my strange feeling, but one of the seneschals stepped forward and announced, "Court is now adjourned!"

King Arthur rose from his seat and strolled through the parting crowd. People bowed deeply as he passed, heading toward the doors.

Anna started to follow the crowd that followed the king, so I fell in right behind her. Houdain caught up and walked silently beside me.

"You don't have to come," I said.

"Yes, I do," he replied.

The crowd dispersed outside the great hall, and we spotted

King Arthur strolling toward the gardens with a few nobles. We followed him from a great distance, allowing a lot of people to walk between us. The closer we got to the gardens, the stranger I felt. That sense of something falling on me grew, as did a sense of . . . *power*, a tingling feeling like lightning was about to strike nearby.

At the entrance to the gardens, Arthur turned slightly, his gaze pointed directly at us. Even from this far away, he knew what we were up to. We stopped walking.

"He looks angry," Anna said quietly.

"We need to do this, no matter what," I said.

Anna was thoughtful for a moment, then said, "What if we were invisible?"

"That might work. Have you ever performed an invisibility spell before?" I had never attempted one, but maybe Anna had in Avalon.

Anna shook her head. "But I've studied the incantations for it."

"Of course you have," I said with good-natured sarcasm.

"What's that supposed to mean?" she asked with a huff, having misunderstood my sarcasm.

"I didn't mean it like it was a bad thing," I said quickly. "I meant that of course you would have already read about most spells. You study all the time." Her shoulders relaxed slightly, but she still had an eyebrow lifted, head cocked to the side, so I said, "It's something I've learned to expect from you. You're . . . handy."

Anna rolled her eyes. "It requires ingredients. We can get them from Master Merlin's study."

A large warm hand gently took my elbow, causing me to turn around. Anna did too, and we found Mordred smiling at us.

"Strolling the garden before dinner?" he said, completely

sincere and calm. Happy, in fact.

I laughed loudly at him to hide my terror. It was a failed attempt to act casually. Anna kept her poise, though, and replied, "It's so beautiful, we just can't get enough. Are you going that way too?"

"In fact, I am," Mordred said. He kept his hand on my elbow and steered me forward. He seemed hyperfocused on me but nodded his head, indicating Anna and the others should follow. Anna had to because of our bond, but my heart jumped into my throat from the brave and determined expression on Houdain's face. He wouldn't leave me alone with this monster, even if Mordred could crush him.

I couldn't stop focusing on Mordred's touch. My elbow burned from the inside, but not in a burning skin, impending death sort of way. It was gentle. A slow heat.

I glanced at Houdain again. He stared straight ahead, almost too stiffly. He held his head high and didn't turn it to watch people or grin at them like he usually did. I took a breath to say something to him that would make him laugh but held it when Mordred's voice spoke in my ear. "There is something in the garden I'd like to show you."

"Me?" I squeaked.

Anna's eyes met mine. They were full of questions, probably like the ones racing in my own mind. Did Mordred know we'd broken his enchantment? Had he tracked us down to respell us? Or worse?

"The both of you," he said. "I think you two will like them." He took his mouth away from my ear, though he kept hold of my elbow, and the sudden absence of the heat from his breath made me shiver.

King Arthur turned down a garden path, and I took a step in that direction, but then Mordred gently squeezed my elbow. "It's down that way," he said, steering me in the opposite direction.

The tingling came back, and I shivered in response. I would have written it off as fear, but I could feel the magic of it. Was it my magic, Mordred's magic, or something else entirely? I tried to shake the feeling off, but it was persistent, so I ignored it as best I could as Mordred led us forward.

Khalid positioned himself to walk slightly in front of Anna and right next to Mordred.

Anna asked, "What is it you want to show us, Lord Mordred?"

"Up here. I had it brought from far away. The people in the south of Iberia call it Ḥabb el-fahm. It means 'seed of understanding.' "

Hearing the definition from Mordred suddenly intensified the tingling in my body. What was going on?

We continued walking around the perimeter of the garden until Mordred said, "Here we are." Up ahead were several plants in large clay pots. They were about a foot tall, with each plant having four or five shoots climbing stiffly toward the sky. The leaves were bright green, and the small flowers were yellowish green with light green stamens. Taken all together, the plants were bright and attractive.

I nearly tripped. The tingling had now turned into full-blown vibrating. I glanced at my hands, sure I'd find them shaking uncontrollably, but they were calm and steady. It appeared the tingling was all internal.

The sensation calmed down enough for me to hide it from Mordred. I focused on the plants to distract myself. They didn't stand out from any of the others in the garden, but I was drawn to them unexplainably. "It's a medicine?" I guessed.

Mordred let go of my elbow and strode to the plants. He said, "That's correct. I heard that eating parts of the plant improves the memory. Or even with a touch."

He *knew*. Without question. And he had taken us to this plant to force us to admit that we'd broken his spell. Maybe he thought we'd used this plant to break the enchantment.

Not sure how I should play this, I took a deep breath. "Our memories are fine, Lord Mordred," I said carefully.

Anna, apparently, wanted to keep up the ruse as she asked with a forced friendliness, "How did you learn about it? I've never seen it mentioned in any of my books."

Mordred picked off a flower from the plant and gently brushed my cheek with it. I instinctively flinched, but the tingling in my body nearly made me faint. I shook my head to snap out of it, thankfully with success.

A crook of a smile, then he moved closer to Anna, making Khalid's temple twitch. Mordred shrugged. "Your books were written by people who have never left this part of the world, priestess. There are new trade routes to places you could never dream of."

"I'm betting you've never left this part of the world either," I said.

"No. But I learn. I listen. I talk to people. Much like I'm doing right now. This world is full of people with ideas different from ours. Compared to most of them, England is still . . . primitive." He indicated the plants with a gesture and pocketed the flower. His eyes met mine. "Do you like them?"

"They are interesting, Lord Mordred, but I still don't understand why they are for us." He'd have to admit we'd broken his spell because I wasn't budging.

Houdain chimed in, nearly growling, "I know all about the ⊠abb el-fahm, Lord Mordred."

Mordred's eyebrow went up. "Do you, Houdain?"

"I do. It's poisonous. Very. If you survive, your memory improves." Every word he spoke was like an accusation. He slowly stepped in front of me. "You can use it for trances too. But again, you have to survive."

I put my hand on Houdain's arm and gently tugged him back. I took a deep, calming breath. "Really?" I said innocently. "I've heard about trances and have always wanted to try one. But they're advanced magic."

Anna stepped up beside me in a protective stance, which took me by surprise. "It was very kind of you to think of us, Lord Mordred. This was . . . thoughtful. Very exotic."

"I must admit, I had Bronwyn in mind when I chose it. The plant also helps with concentration, and there is no plant like it here that has the effectiveness." Mordred moved closer to me. "You and I are alike, Priestess Bronwyn. Magic flows through us. I know what it's like to fight back the power of it."

His power radiated off of him the closer he stood to me. It was palpable and strong. But what was more frightening was the fact that it felt . . . like me.

"It's getting late, Bronwyn," Anna announced. "We have dinner with Merlin tonight." We weren't having dinner with Merlin. We were to have dinner with the king. I was about to correct her when Anna took my arm and tugged several times, like a little child. "We have to get ready or we'll be late." It was the tugging that got through to me that something was wrong and we had to get away from there. I let her pull me away. Houdain and Khalid fell in right behind us.

Once we were out of sight of Mordred and it was clear he wasn't following us, Anna said quietly, her voice shaking with her rapid steps, "I think he spelled you, Bronwyn. We need to get back to our rooms right away so I can check."

"I'm not under a spell. I'm fine." I was fine. Completely. Of course, I'd thought I was fine when I *was* under a spell, but I didn't think anything was wrong now. Even the tingling was subsiding.

"I need to make sure," Anna insisted. "And we need to hurry."

"She's right, Bronwyn," Houdain said from behind us. "You were acting weird."

"I was not!" I said.

"You were kinda sparkling," Houdain said.

I stopped walking and turned. "I was *not* sparkling." But I'd been tingling. A lot. So maybe I had been. "Was I?"

Still holding my arm, Anna exerted as much force as she could to move us toward the staircase. "He definitely knows we broke his memory-wiping spell. It's no coincidence he showed us a plant that improves memory. He was taunting us. And then you went all strange, like you were in love or something."

Houdain moved in closer to Bronwyn, then said defensively, "I wouldn't say *love*. She just looked confused."

"*Love?* Mordred? More like terrified. I was sure he would try to cast another memory-wiping spell on us right there! But it also means that if *we* were with *him*, he couldn't do anything to the king." I thought for another moment. "I *was* feeling this tingling thing all over me while we were there though. It was intense."

"See? I was right," Anna replied. "And we need to hurry. King Arthur might have been safe while we were with Mordred, but he's not safe now. We'll have to wait until dinner if we don't want to cause suspicion. I hope Mordred doesn't try anything in the next hour."

Back in our room, Anna checked me for spells. "Nothing," she said with a sigh. "You're totally clean, at least as far as I can tell."

"But I was sparkling?"

"Not a lot," Houdain said from across the room. He leaned on the wall near the window. "But I noticed."

There was a knock at the door.

We all exchanged surprised glances.

Khalid took the initiative and answered the door.

A young page stood with his chest puffed out. "King Arthur requests your presence at his private dining hall this evening." With that, he bowed and left.

"Private dining hall? Not the main dining hall? That might work to our advantage. Not as big a space to guard. Let's get there early, make sure everything is safe for the king," I said, wanting to direct the conversation away from my *sparkling*.

"Good idea." Anna nodded, and we all left the room once more.

The halls were practically empty as the residents prepared for the nightly meal. When we had been in the gardens, the swollen clouds had warned us of what was to come. Rain fell, coming down in sheets outside the windows.

Like every night since we'd arrived, we were having dinner with King Arthur and whichever group of nobles Arthur had chosen for the evening. But we'd only been to his private hall twice.

We turned a corner, and I had to stop. The tingling feeling had started again. "It's happening again. That tingling feeling," I said. "Am I sparkling?"

Houdain shook his head.

"Do you think Mordred is nearby?" Anna whispered to me.

We inspected the area as much as we could. Houdain stood awkwardly near me, and Khalid was nowhere to be found, which meant he was somewhere close to us. He obviously didn't feel like we were in danger or he'd have been attached to Anna's side in an instant.

I shook my head. "Maybe it's a residual feeling from the garden."

"Maybe." Anna glanced over her shoulder cautiously. "We'll have to be more observant than we thought. I have a bad feeling."

"Me too," I said.

In response to our growing feeling of doom, we nearly ran the rest of the way to the private dining hall, where a knight stood at attention and opened the door for us. Khalid, as a guard, stood just inside the doorway, his eyes trained on our every move.

The hall was large, but it was a closet compared to the great hall. The ceiling was high and tapered to a point. A beautiful copper candelabrum hung from it; its dozens of candles lit the room, perfectly casting a yellow glow on the giant round wooden table. Houdain had informed me the first time we had dinner here that this wasn't *the* Round Table. *That* table resided in Arthur's war room and was off-limits. But this table was majestic all the same, with its decorative carved pedestal underneath. The chairs were as intricately designed as the table, with high backs and dark stained wood. I always felt like a noble myself sitting in such luxury.

We were the first to arrive and searched the room for anything suspicious.

"I don't see anything nefarious," Anna said as a few nobles trickled in.

My vision swam for a moment as the tingling intensified. I whispered to Anna, "Am I sparkling now?"

She eyed me over quickly, then shook her head.

With a quick search, there was still no sign of Mordred.

"Welcome," King Arthur announced from the doorway, which startled both Anna and me. "Please come and sit." The remaining nobles followed Arthur into the hall, sitting at their respective seats.

He glanced our way and gave us a small nod. Whatever he thought about us earlier was not there now, at least not that I could see.

We sat at our chairs, and a servant brought us cups of wine. I peered inside. I'd never seen wine so red. It was almost like blood.

"It isn't poisoned, I assure you," Arthur said and then laughed. "It is called Barolo. From Byzantium."

"Thank you, my lord," Anna said. "Did you travel there?"

"My son gave it to me as a gift."

Of course he did.

Mordred still hadn't arrived, which made me more worried.

Servants began bringing in enormous amounts of food on large silver trays, from roasted ham, to legs of lamb, to breads and cheeses. The dishes came out so quickly that I couldn't possibly keep track. I knew there was no possible way the people sitting here would finish all this food. What a waste. I made a quick prayer to the Goddess that the kitchen staff would give the leftovers to the poor.

The delicious aroma filled my nostrils, and it wasn't until that moment I realized how hungry I was.

"A toast." King Arthur stood and lifted his cup. As one, everyone in the room followed his lead and stood, lifting their drinks in turn.

He tipped his cup toward us. "To Anna and Bronwyn, priestesses of Avalon. You've only been here a few short weeks, but Merlin tells me you've excelled at your studies beyond his expectations."

My toes curled. Merlin had said that? I could see the king's words affected Anna as well, as she sat a little straighter and her chin slightly lifted.

"This is tremendous opportunity for Avalon to rekindle its relationship with more of England," King Arthur said. "For centuries, the priestesses have only spoken to the high kings. This is the reason you two are here, although none of us expected it would be this soon . . ." The king motioned for us to sit, which we did. We were at the opposite end of the table from him. "I am worried about England's future. I think wars are coming. Merlin hasn't denied it. And to survive, I believe we need to strengthen the bonds amongst our own people before outsiders invade again."

I didn't want to be the one to tell him that Avalon would never fight in a war. Who was I to question the king or anger him any more than I already had?

He continued as if reading my thoughts. "Avalon is a magical force of nature that symbolizes everything about England that has been forgotten by the people who are in positions of power and influence. Reminding everyone that Avalon has been watching and has returned to the world to reteach the people what it truly means to be 'of England' will unite us, no matter our differences. And don't worry, priestesses, if I ever did expect Avalon to fight, I would not ask for it to interfere until war is inevitable. I want to avoid war as much as I am able."

And that was why Arthur was the greatest high king in the history of England.

I took another sip of wine, and the tingling sensation hit me hard and fast. I shivered.

Anna stared at me, wide-eyed.

"What is happening to you, Priestess Bronwyn?" Arthur asked, rising to his feet.

I jumped up from my seat as well, seeing little sparkles all over me. The tingling was overpowering, like a blanket covering my entire body.

Crack!

What was that?

That wasn't me!

The sound echoed off every surface.

My vision swam, and everything began to blur. My knees buckled, and I started to fall to the ground. Just before I hit stone, Anna leapt out of her seat and jumped on the table itself, headed toward Arthur.

The copper candelabrum was falling.

And it was about to crush the king.

Chapter 13
ANNA

Oh. My. Goddess.

I was so focused on Bronwyn becoming a shimmering star that the loud snap from above my head didn't translate as danger.

Until the copper candelabrum dropped at a frightening speed and fell straight toward . . .

King Arthur.

Leaping onto the table and lifting my robe, I ran faster than I'd ever run in my life.

But I was going to be too late.

I wasn't fast enough.

A quick incantation fixed that, causing my feet to move three times their normal speed.

Reaching Arthur mere seconds before the copper monstrosity made contact, I hurled my body against his, throwing us both to the floor.

Crack!

The candelabrum smashed King Arthur's chair as if it were made of twigs.

And suddenly I was face-to-face with the king himself, sprawled on top of him in the most embarrassing way possible.

Chaos ensued behind us: screams from the guests at the table, boots rushing toward us, the last of the chair smashing to bits as the candelabrum finally settled to the stone floor.

Arthur eyed his demolished chair next to us, then carefully pulled me off his chest while saying, "You saved my life, Priestess Anna. I am in your debt."

Sir Gawain and Sir Lancelot reached our sides and helped us to our feet. They were a lot more concerned about Arthur's well-being than mine, but that was to be expected.

King Arthur gently pushed the two knights away and reached out, taking both my hands in his. "Are you hurt?"

"No, I'm fine. Thank you, Your Majesty. I'm simply grateful that I made it to you in time," I answered, though I couldn't hide the shake in my hands as he let go of them.

Khalid rushed to my side. Though he had to hide his feelings for me, he didn't have to hide that he was a priestess of Avalon's guard. "Are you sure you aren't hurt, Priestess Anna? I was too far back to help you." His eyes revealed the pain it took to admit that.

I wanted to wrap my arms around him, but I brushed my robe with my hands and said, "I assure you, I am fine, Khalid. There was nothing you could do. I had to use magic to speed up my feet to reach the king."

Bronwyn was at my side too, no longer sparkling. "Majesty, something magical was at play. I don't think the candelabrum falling was an accident."

Sir Gawain inspected the chain of the candelabrum; it was

broken. He turned to Arthur. "The links are worn. No magic was used; it was simply shoddy copperwork. We should have the smith who forged these chains brought in for punishment."

I wasn't sure if that was true or not. Gawain knew about Mordred's plans, but he was adamantly against them according to what Bronwyn had overheard that day. Had he changed his mind? Was he covering for Mordred? Or was he planning on handling Mordred himself? The only magic I sensed had come from Bronwyn, and it hadn't been directed at the candelabrum at all. I needed to talk to her in private. She seemed so sure that magic had been used.

"Your Majesty, *magic* can wear through a chain. It would appear the same either way, whether from shoddy craftmanship or a metal-weakening spell." I kept my voice calm and steady.

Bronwyn's eyes met mine, and there was genuine gratitude there. She had probably expected me to side with Gawain. We may have had our differences privately, but she was a priestess of Avalon, and I'd always have her back, even if I wanted to push it sometimes.

Mordred strode in and arrived at our sides, sighing heavily. "Let me guess. You both think *I* had something to do with this?"

Now that he'd *said* it, it would make us appear paranoid. He wasn't even hiding that he knew we'd broken his memory spell anymore, referring to when we'd first accused him of poisoning his father. Smart. I hated him.

Bronwyn was obviously tired of playing games and pretending we were still under his spell. She spoke her mind. "Yes, we do think you did it. I felt your magic in the garden, and I felt it here. Exactly the same. Like a signature. I have zero doubt that you caused this to happen."

Mordred cast his eyes down as if he were hurt by the accusation.

Such a performer. "Like I said, Father. It seems their kindness to me in these last few weeks was fleeting, and now they've gone back to distrusting me again. I don't know what I can do to make these priestesses see that I am only a devoted son and not the monster they seem to think I am."

I wanted to cast some kind of impotence spell on him.

Arthur shook his head. His expression wasn't one of betrayal; it was one of irritancy and a little bit of sympathy.

"Khalid, please escort the priestesses back to their chambers," Arthur ordered

Bronwyn's nostrils flared, and she focused back on King Arthur. "Your Majesty, I know you don't want to believe your own son is capable of such things, but I heard him. He wants you dead." She motioned to the crushed chair. "And if it hadn't been for Anna, he would have gotten his wish."

"Enough!" Arthur yelled.

The room went silent.

Bronwyn lowered her head, and her hands shook. She was scared, and strangely, all I wanted to do was comfort her.

Arthur motioned Gawain to his side. "Please help Khalid take these girls to their chambers."

With that, Arthur left the room, followed by Sir Lancelot, Houdain, and Mordred, but not before Mordred discreetly winked at me.

Winked!

The bastard.

Literally.

Khalid eyed Sir Gawain with suspicion, but I knew it was probably more out of worry for my safety and Bronwyn's. But maybe it wasn't. Maybe he saw something we couldn't. Gawain knew about Mordred's plans and had basically declared him innocent; that was definitely a reason to question Gawain's intentions.

Standing between Gawain and the two of us, Khalid made sure that the knight kept his distance. The strange part was that Sir Gawain didn't speak. He simply marched next to Khalid, staring straight ahead with little to no expression on his face.

Something was off.

As we walked through the hallways, heading toward our room, I touched Bronwyn's hand to grab her attention.

She jumped at my touch. Her eyes met mine, and my heart squeezed with sympathy. Given her tense jaw and watery eyes, I could tell she was holding back tears. Her expression was almost defiant, as if she expected me to rub her failure in, as if I thought it actually was a failure.

I couldn't blame her. It wasn't as if I'd ever given her any reason to believe that I *wouldn't* play the blame game in a situation like this, despite me supporting her publicly with the king.

After the king shut us down, she *had* persisted when she shouldn't have. *Read the room, Bronwyn.* Feeling my temper begin to rise, I took a deep, calming breath and gave a quick nod toward Gawain.

Bronwyn's features relaxed slightly when I didn't attack her. She glanced briefly at Gawain, then mouthed to me, "What do you think?"

"I think something is off," I mouthed back.

Though our voices weren't even a whisper, Gawain's head twisted unnaturally toward us, like his own body wasn't under his control.

Gooseflesh rose on my arms and legs.

I decided to pretend that I wasn't terrified, though my heart

152

raced uncontrollably. "Can I help you?" I said with as much snark as I could, not sure if I had hidden the quake in my voice.

Without answering, Gawain turned his head back to its forward position.

What was that? Bronwyn's voice sounded inside my head.

Um.

Can you hear me? I tentatively asked in my brain, feeling a bit like a crazy person.

Bronwyn jumped like she had when I had touched her hand. *Yes. Did you cast a spell?* She appeared as shocked as I was.

Did you hear *me cast a spell?* Again with the snark.

Why are you the worst? Bronwyn groaned, and I could physically feel the groan.

Sorry. You're right. This is actually a good thing. You probably did it accidentally because you're so volatile and can't control your magic.

Bronwyn rolled her eyes. *Thanks.*

You know what I mean. My point is it's good we can communicate. I wished I knew how long it would last. Since Bronwyn had no control over her magic, this conversation could end abruptly. I needed to take advantage of it as long as it lasted. *Something's wrong with Sir Gawain. Did you see that twisting head move?*

Yeah. Spell? You think Mordred is controlling him? Bronwyn asked what I had been fearing.

If it is a spell, we'll have to figure out a way to counter it if he . . . you know, tries something. Maybe Mordred wanted to keep an eye on us, still holding back from hurting us because *Avalon* might kick his butt.

If he's willing to kill the king, he's willing to kill priestesses.

Oh, dang. She'd heard that.

I can hear everything.

153

Well, stop!

Don't think of anything embarrassing, I thought. *Don't think of anything embarrassing.* I thought of that time I tried to spy on Khalid and tripped and fell off the retaining wall.

Bronwyn burst out laughing.

Khalid and Gawain turned toward her with surprise.

Ugh.

Fine. You can hear everything. Can we figure out what we're going to do?

Nothing.

Silence.

Bronwyn's eyes met mine, and they were tinged with panic and disappointment. Our telepathic connection was gone.

At least we'd been able to share our suspicion of Gawain. It had served some purpose anyway. And now we'd both be on guard. My only regret was not asking what had happened when she went all sparkly in the dining hall. Did she know what had caused that? Had it been Mordred trying to control her? I had so many questions, but now our line of communication was closed until we could enter our room and get some distance from Sir Gawain.

Reaching over, I squeezed her hand in support, and she squeezed back.

After traversing the last staircase, we finally reached our floor and walked toward the large oak doors that led to our room and somehow signified safety in my head. I fully planned on pulling Khalid and Bronwyn inside and slamming the door on Gawain. Distance. That was as good a strategy as any.

But as we grew closer and closer to the door, the gooseflesh on my arms flared up once more.

Something was about to happen.

Khalid's hand slowly moved toward the hilt of his sheathed sword. He must have sensed it too.

Only ten more paces.

Sir Gawain marched forward, seemingly oblivious to his surroundings.

Eight more paces. Almost there.

Khalid's hand tightened around the hilt.

Six more paces.

Bronwyn's hand squeezed tighter, the tingling of her magic pumping through her touch.

Four more paces.

Three.

Two.

One.

Grabbing the door with my free hand, I swung it open and then hurried inside with Bronwyn and Khalid. I let go of Bronwyn's hand, and we all turned to face Sir Gawain.

But he simply stood there.

Doing nothing.

He didn't try to enter.

He didn't try to attack.

He stood a foot away from the doorframe and stared straight ahead. Weird, but not dangerous.

Maybe he *was* there to spy.

I carefully began pushing the doors closed.

With a loud *shwank*, Sir Gawain's sword left its scabbard and slammed down toward my head.

A long blade immediately appeared in front of my face, blocking Gawain's sword from slicing me in two.

Khalid used the force of his body and pushed it into the blade to move Gawain back, throwing the knight off-balance.

"Don't kill him!" Bronwyn shouted.

Adjusting his stance to defense instead of offense, Khalid nodded. "If Sir Gawain is under a spell, I suggest you break it."

I couldn't have agreed more.

Gawain leapt to his feet and swung at Khalid viciously, clumsily; that wasn't the stuff knights were made of. Lucky for us, it only made it easier for Khalid to keep the knight back.

No one on our floor seemed to notice or care that there was a sword fight clanging around them. But then again, if Mordred had set all this up, he would have cleared the floor anyway. Or spelled them asleep. I wanted to kick myself for not preparing properly for Mordred's wickedness. We'd underestimated him.

Bronwyn turned to me. "Can you get inside Gawain's head? See if he's spelled like you did with all of us and the memory spell?"

We ducked as Gawain's sword came dangerously close to our heads, but Khalid fought like a man possessed, and if I hadn't been terrified, I'd have been swooning.

Concentrate.

"I can't concentrate with *that!*" I gestured wildly toward the two men fighting viciously.

Swoosh!

That had almost hit Khalid's shoulder.

I needed this to end.

"You have to!" Bronwyn spoke loudly but calmly. "I can't do it as precisely as you can. I need you, Anna. Khalid needs you." It was a plea, and Bronwyn never pleaded.

I had to do this.

Concentrate.

I closed my eyes.

After a moment, I could feel the strong thread of connection between me and Sir Gawain. I was almost in. Focusing harder, my mind traveled into his. The clanking and swooshing of swords threatened to break my concentration, but I needed to do this to save us all. No pressure at all.

But there was nothing.

His mind was clear.

No spell.

My eyes flew open and met Bronwyn's. "There's nothing there. No spell has been cast."

"Impossible." Bronwyn's face paled as if stricken. We turned back to the raging fight as Sir Gawain swung wide, missing Khalid entirely. The knight's eyes were still glazed over.

I stared in disbelief. "He looks *wrong*."

"You must have missed something," Bronwyn said.

Seeing her expression of utter despair, I knew it wasn't an accusation; it was a declaration of helplessness.

"I swear I didn't. There's no spell, unless it's so hidden that I can't find it." I hated admitting I might have failed, but it was a possibility we had to consider.

With an underhanded shove to the knees, Sir Gawain finally knocked Khalid to the ground, gaining access . . . to us.

"Brace yourself," Bronwyn announced with such force in her voice that a chill raced down my spine. "Incant the shield spell."

Gawain charged forward, sword held over his head, ready to strike us down.

Right.

Shield.

The words spilled out of my mouth as if I recited them every day, and Bronwyn's innate magic strengthened each word.

The sword swung down.

And bounced off the magic shield as if it were made of hard metal.

Gawain fell back from the shock of it, which gave Khalid enough time to counter the next attack.

Sir Gawain wasn't going to stop.

He was going to keep coming until we were dead.

Chapter 14
BRONWYN

Sir Gawain was like the walking dead. His eyes were . . . empty. His face had no expression. Nothing. It was as if he wore a mask as he swung his long, narrow sword over his head to bring it down hard on our shield.

Again, the sword bounced off.

As he raised it yet again, he suddenly swung his body around to deflect Khalid's attack. And Khalid, for all his *amazing* speed and skill, was not expecting it. Gawain's body slammed into Khalid's, and our protector flew backward against the wall.

Anna's face crumpled in terror, and I could feel her concentration on the shield spell slip.

Gawain regained his balance quickly, turning on his heel back toward us.

From somewhere down the hallway came a bellowing the likes of which I had never heard before. It was . . . warbly?

And there he was!

Houdain.

He ran full speed toward Sir Gawain, sword overhead and ready to smash.

Anna started toward Khalid, but I put my arm in front of her.

"Let me go!" she growled at me, but I wasn't about to do that. I'd seen many battles. It seemed like Britain was always being invaded. The Romans had left a couple centuries before I was born, and the Saxons had been raiding ever since. One might think that sword fights involved quick, clanging movements that anyone would be silly trying to dodge, but that wasn't how they really happened. These swords were heavy and long. The only reason they were balanced in anyone's hand was because of a big round knob at the end of the handle. They were sharp, too, but hardly anyone was killed by cutting or jabbing. It was more like you died from being crushed on the head or having your legs chopped off. So sword "fights" were more like sword . . . avoidings? They were deceptively slow movements.

While I tried to hold Anna back, our protective shield began to disappear.

Khalid valiantly climbed back to his feet.

Houdain ran awkwardly, gloriously at what I knew would be a fatal blow from Sir Gawain's sword.

My mind froze in terror, and my body clamped up, stiff as stone.

Sir Gawain began to glow.

Was anyone seeing this?

"Anna, Sir Gawain is sparkling . . ."

A deep, guttural scream built inside my body, and before I could hold it back, it escaped from my mouth.

***

A tapping on my cheek. Someone's hand.

Anna's.

"Bronwyn. Wake up."

After some effort, I opened my eyes. Everything was too bright and out of focus. But I could see the shadow of Anna's face, and her hair glowed gold from a light behind her.

She looked . . . magical.

I tried to sit up on my own. Bad idea. Fortunately, two hands behind me helped. The light behind Anna was fire from a candle sconce on the far wall. The candles were all lit. I knew we'd just had dinner, but the sun wasn't supposed to set for another hour. Was it night already? How long had I been unconscious?

Examining the area more thoughtfully, I noticed that late afternoon light shone through the upper windows. It was hazy from the continuing rainfall and the coming sunset.

Khalid walked around lighting the last of the candles.

"What did I do?" I asked. My voice sounded far away.

Houdain said from behind me, "You stopped Sir Gawain."

"And you blocked out the light from the windows," Anna said, her eyes glimmering.

Was she *proud* of me?

Gawain lay peacefully on the floor nearby.

"Is he dead?" I asked.

Khalid kneeled beside the knight. "No, Priestess Bronwyn. But he is in a deep sleep, and we must move him from the hallway as soon as possible."

"Can you sit up on your own?" Houdain asked, his breath tickling my ear. Oh boy. Even in this state, all I could do was nod.

Houdain stood up and lifted Gawain's body with ease, carrying the knight inside our room.

"What exactly did I do, Anna?"

She shook her head. "All I know is that you said Gawain was sparkling, and then you screamed, and this ball of . . . something . . . mist? Like a black mist. It shot out of you and expanded, and then the windows were covered in darkness, and I felt myself fall over."

"I'm so sorry—"

"Don't be, Bronwyn. I was fine. I just fell over. Khalid found all the sconces and lit the candles. It's almost nighttime anyway. Then we saw you and Sir Gawain lying on the floor . . . sparkling."

"Sparkling. Like before?"

"Yes, but more intense."

"Oh my goddess. You're right. He's not under a spell. Not exactly," I responded.

"What do you mean?"

"That herb Mordred showed us in the garden. What was it called?"

"*Habb el-fahm.*"

"That's got to be it, Anna. This whole sparkling business started in the garden and intensified when Mordred touched my cheek with the flower. It must have activated it or something because of my innate magic mixed with his or something? I don't know. It has to be connected somehow. But Houdain, you said it can put people in trances too. Sir Gawain was as tranced as they come, right?"

Anna nodded in agreement. "Then we'd better make sure Sir Gawain can't come after us again if he wakes up and is still being affected by it."

"I don't have any idea how to do that. Do you?"

"Well, no. Not yet. But at least we can tie him down until we do."

With the help of Khalid, who was only mildly bruised from

the collision with the wall, thank the Goddess, we used our bedding to tie Sir Gawain, his body a stiff board, and lay him on one of the couches in our room.

Once he awoke and we were sure Gawain couldn't break free, the four of us focused on a cure.

Houdain was the first to speak. "The books say if you eat too many seeds, you die."

Anna sighed. "And it's not like we can be sure Mordred didn't give him too many. Sir Gawain knew of Mordred's plans to kill Arthur. Mordred would want Sir Gawain dead. He probably thought Khalid would finish him off back there before the seeds did."

"We have to get the seeds out of him somehow," Khalid said.

"We need to make him vomit," I suggested.

Houdain said, "I'm not sticking my finger down his throat."

Anna said, "We need something from the medic."

Houdain hurried out to find the medic for Camelot. He would make up a story that one of us had eaten something bad and refused to see anyone but him.

Meanwhile, Khalid returned to his post right outside our door, leaving Anna and me to watch over Sir Gawain, who quietly struggled against his bonds.

"I'm so relieved you figured it out," Anna said.

"What do you mean?"

"The herb. I was sure it was some spell that we weren't powerful enough to break. You might have saved his life."

"Well, you knew to go to the medic. I didn't know there was a medicine to make you vomit."

Anna smiled slightly. "Yeah. We worked together, didn't we?"

"Looks that way." I shook my head, still in shock.

"It was very heroic of you to black out the windows when you saw Houdain was in trouble." A slight tug of the corner of Anna's mouth indicated that she was teasing me. But I wasn't ready to admit my feelings about that.

"I would have done that for anyone."

"Ha!"

"I would!"

"Anyway, what are we going to do?" she asked seriously.

"About what?"

"Mordred! We stopped him this time, but what about the next? He wants the king dead. He wants *us* dead. We should talk to Arthur again."

"He doesn't believe us, Anna. You know that."

"Then Merlin." Her eyes shifted frantically.

"He said we had to stay out of it or we'll get kicked out of Camelot."

"I'd rather get *kicked out* of Camelot than die!" Anna practically shrieked.

I nodded. "You're right. He'll have to do something now."

Anna opened her mouth to respond, but I didn't get to hear what she was going to say.

I wasn't in our room anymore.

I was . . . I didn't know. I felt as if I were in a room, but I couldn't see any walls, just bright lights all around, different colors shifting almost too slow to perceive.

And Merlin. He stood as close to me as Anna had been, his dark robes seeming even darker in this light.

"We must work on your self-control," he said. "You are extremely lucky your explosive enchantment only affected a small area, and not one involving the king."

164

"I'm so sorry, Merlin. I—"

He put up a hand to stop me. "I know what happened, Bronwyn. You don't need to explain it to me. And what matters is that you did well. You hurt no one, damaged nothing, and saved several. You *will* learn to control your power, and when you do, you might even surpass me."

"I . . ." I had no words. I knew it was a compliment, but the chill in my bones made it feel like a death sentence.

"Now, listen carefully. You must remember our conversation beyond this space."

"Where are we?"

"You are still in your room, and I am in mine. We are living within a single moment of time."

"It's beautiful."

"Yes, and we can discuss that later, but you must focus on what I'm about to tell you. Mordred must be stopped. I thought I could handle him on my own, but he is much more powerful than I originally suspected. I can't stop him alone. You both must go to the great hall quickly."

Would it be rude to say *I told you so*? I decided against it considering how dire the situation was.

"What about Sir Gawain?"

"Houdain will return to your room shortly to administer the emetic—"

"The what?"

Merlin took a deep breath, as if trying to calm himself, and then answered, "It will make Gawain vomit. He'll recover and remember nothing." His face was suddenly directly in front of mine, his eyes intense and . . . scared? "Go quickly!"

And there I was again, staring at Anna, shivers racing down

my spine at the intensity of meeting with Merlin.

Anna finished her thought as if I hadn't left time and space. "Then let's go find Merlin now!"

"I did already!" I cried louder than I'd expected. "I was just with him! He needs our help! He wants us to help now!" I was too frazzled and excited to keep it in.

"What are you talking about?"

Houdain burst through the doors with a vial in his hand. "Got it!"

"Just like Merlin said." I grabbed Anna's hand and pulled her to the door.

"What is happening, Bronwyn?" Anna asked as she came willingly with me to the hallway, Khalid our shadow.

"Hey, where are you going?" Houdain called from our room.

I yelled back, "Make Sir Gawain vomit, then meet us in the great hall!"

A kind of hiccupped yelp came from Houdain.

Anna's eyes met mine, and they were wide with fear and wonder as we hurried toward the great hall.

I explained, "Merlin contacted me and said he needs our help to defeat Mordred."

She swallowed hard and nodded, grip tightening in mine.

I knew how she felt.

What were we running toward that the great Merlin couldn't handle alone?

Chapter 15
ANNA

Heart racing, we ran toward Arthur and his impending doom. I prayed to the Goddess that we weren't too late. Khalid's shoulders were my only view as we made our way through the winding hallways since he had positioned himself in front of us. I knew he was doing it to protect us, but if we were about to face Mordred, it would be with magic, not brute force. I knew Khalid wanted to be our bodyguard, but my stomach twisted with the knowledge that it would probably end up the other way around.

But I'd protect him with my life.

So he'd better not do anything stupid or valiant.

My stomach sank further as I knew with certainty that Khalid would *absolutely* do something stupid *and* valiant. I'd have to make sure he didn't get hurt.

Almost there.

I was surprised that we ran toward the great hall without taking any wrong turns. My mind had obviously kept track of the fortress's layout even in the short time we'd stayed here.

"Hey, wait up!" Houdain's voice came from behind us.

We didn't stop, but Houdain's long legs allowed him to finally catch up, keeping pace with Bronwyn.

Our small group rounded the last corner, and the ceiling rose up above us as we entered the main corridor that led to the great hall.

Merlin stood before the closed double doors but hurried toward us as we approached. To say it was alarming to see the most powerful wizard in the world rush to our sides was an understatement. Things would have to be very dire for Merlin to need our help, especially after expressly telling us to stay out of it. What could two priestesses-in-training do that he couldn't?

Block out the *windows*. Empty a *lake* to put out a self-caused *forest fire!*

I may have been good at spellcasting, but Bronwyn was a force that rivaled any magician.

That scared me to my core but also gave me a small hope that we might be able to defeat Mordred and whatever he had planned.

When Merlin reached our sides, he turned to us. "Do you two feel it?"

I wasn't sure what he meant, but Bronwyn nodded solemnly, and I suddenly felt as if I were failing a lesson in school.

Admitting it seemed like the best course of action, though, because I truly felt nothing except the rising bile in my stomach. "I don't feel anything, Master Merlin."

Bronwyn answered though. "Magic. Very powerful. It's pulsing."

Pulsing?

Nope. Definitely none of that.

Merlin nodded in appreciation and approval, which again made my stomach twist. We were about to fight Mordred or something magical, and I was jealous? I needed to pull it together. Bronwyn was an innate magic user, and I was not. This would of course give her senses I did not possess, but why did it hurt my ego so much?

Shockingly, Bronwyn didn't give me a smug or superior look, as I'd fully expected her to. Instead, she grabbed my hand again. "Use a sensor spell. You'll be able to feel it through me."

Inclusion? We'd come a lot further in our relationship than I could have ever imagined. Maybe Priestesses Elaine and Florette would sever our magical tie sooner than anyone had expected.

One could hope.

I did as Bronwyn suggested and quickly recited a sensor spell. "Whoa."

"Yeah," Bronwyn said.

It was indeed like a pulsing. Giant bursts of vibration rattled through my body to the point where I thought my teeth would shatter from the force.

Merlin asked me, "You feel it now?"

"Yes." I released myself from the spell to regain my focus. I didn't know how Bronwyn could concentrate on anything feeling waves of magic that strong. It made me wonder if this was why Bronwyn lost control at times; the power was overwhelming. I had a pang of sympathy for her.

"Mordred is summoning something," Merlin said. "Something very big. And if we're right, then he's bringing it here to Camelot to kill his father."

"And King Arthur is in the great hall?" I asked, though it was most certainly a stupid question.

But Merlin answered me without judgment with a nod of his head. "We must hurry inside, even if Arthur orders us to leave. He does not want to see the worst in his son." Merlin motioned for Khalid to sheathe his sword. "We may need brute force, but magic will be our true foe in this battle. Stay back, and only fight if absolutely necessary."

Relief surged through me at Merlin's words. I knew I should've been terrified of what was to come, but hearing Merlin instruct Khalid to hold back flooded me with warmth instead. I also knew that Khalid would completely ignore that advice if any of us were in danger.

Merlin's eyes met Bronwyn's and my own once again. "Hopefully we can settle this before Mordred does any real damage. You two ready?"

We both nodded, though I wasn't ready in the least. I glanced at Bronwyn, and the slight shake in her hands told me she was as scared as I was.

But we were bound.

One.

As much as I didn't like that, we had to make it work for the sake of Arthur and for the sake of the kingdom.

"Houdain, stay behind the girls," Merlin instructed.

Houdain didn't appear happy about that order, but he listened to his master all the same.

Thunder boomed in the distance, rattling wall sconces enough to knock down a candle. The fire snuffed out as it hit the floor, and my skin crawled at the omen.

Without another word, Merlin used magic to open the giant doors of the great hall with a wave of his hand. It would have been impressive at any time, but in this moment, it gave me that extra bit of confidence I needed.

We stepped into the great hall, and King Arthur peered up from where he sat on his throne, a small wooden table perched in front of him with maps strewn on its surface. His head cocked to one side at our group having dramatically stormed in, but he didn't appear angry or suspicious in any way. Aside from him, the enormous room was completely empty.

No Mordred.

No magic.

Just Arthur alone with his maps. He stood up, his expression confused, then said, "Master Merlin. I'm afraid we'll have to speak another time. I agreed to meet Mordred here to go over pressing land disputes. Did I forget a meeting we had scheduled?"

Lightning flashed outside. Its light came through the windows, creating strange shapes on the walls. Thunder followed, this time shaking the floor.

Even I wasn't naïve enough to believe this storm was natural.

But it was Merlin who spoke the words to Arthur. "This storm is magic, Arthur. Designed to destroy. Usually aimed at one person."

Arthur's head reared back with a small laugh. "Master Merlin, I do not want to have this argument again. You've stated how you feel about Mordred, but I think you've been letting yourself be influenced by these two priestesses." He glared at Bronwyn and me. "No disrespect to Avalon, but you two are dangerously close to being tried for treason."

We hadn't known that Merlin had talked to the king about Mordred. I wanted to reach out and hug him, though that would've been entirely inappropriate. Plus, the fact that the king of England was quite possibly going to throw us in a dungeon, or worse, for treason.

Khalid moved closer to me in a protective stance. He served Avalon, not England, so chances were he wouldn't let the high king of England take us or imprison us in any way. My heart beat a little bit faster at having Khalid standing near me.

Thunder boomed again. This time Arthur stumbled slightly. "I'll admit, it's a strong storm, but we've had worse. How could you think Mordred capable of such a thing?"

Merlin stepped closer to the king, his eyes imploring. "Mordred asked to meet. Yet where is he? You are a sitting duck in this room." Merlin stepped closer. "Mordred is a very powerful magician, whether you choose to acknowledge it or not. You speak from a father's point of view, not a king's."

Arthur shook his head. "You are the wisest man I know, Master Merlin, but I believe from the depths of my heart that you are wrong about Mordred."

Lightning struck through a window, hitting a tapestry hanging on the wall. Instantly, it lit on fire, falling to the ground like raining flames. By the time it landed on the cold stone floor, the fire had burnt itself out, leaving only a pile of ashes behind.

Thunder shook the hall once again; this time we all struggled to keep our balance.

Bronwyn clasped my hand again. "Whatever this is, it's coming in fast."

Arthur staggered toward Merlin as another blast of thunder jolted the fortress. "I will never believe this was cast by Mordred, but I have other enemies who use magic." He pulled out his sword. "I will fight anything that tries to harm my people."

Touching Arthur's sword arm, Merlin said, "This storm cannot be fought with mundane weapons. It can only be destroyed by magic."

Bolts of lightning burst through the upper windows and hit the walls, causing sparks to float down toward us.

Bronwyn's hand began to vibrate, but her eyes met Merlin's and not mine. "Merlin! It's coming!"

A black cloud entered with another round of lightning bolts, then slithered down the walls as if it were a snake.

It was alive.

Merlin lifted his hands to cast a spell of protection.

Boom! Crack!

Thunder knocked Merlin to his knees before he could cast his spell, but it didn't stop him. Kneeling, he threw his hands up again just as the largest bolt of lightning so far burst from the black cloud, encasing him in its light. Merlin screamed in pain as the bolt of lightning electrified him over and over.

Light burst out of Bronwyn's chest, surrounding the cocoon of lightning Merlin was wrapped in. The lightning pulled back as if in fear of a more powerful foe, dropping Merlin's body to the ground, unconscious.

The black cloud transformed into a gigantic human-shaped body, well over twenty feet tall. Hundreds of lightning bolts raced around its smoky limbs. It was as if we were witnessing a storm come to life, full of wrath and destruction.

I pushed Houdain toward Arthur with my free hand. "Hide him!"

I wanted to hide *myself*, but holding Bronwyn's hand somehow gave me a sense of bravery I didn't normally feel.

Taking Arthur by the hand, Houdain tugged him toward a table in the back of the room. Arthur shrugged off Houdain's grasp and pointed his sword at the monster. "I fear nothing!" Arthur yelled.

Though the monster's face was made of black smoke with no shape or features, I swore it smiled gleefully at the sound of Arthur's voice. It was as if Arthur was a beacon to the monster as it charged toward him.

Arthur pushed Houdain out of the way, then sidestepped the monster, stabbing it with his sword. But it passed through the creature with no effect. Though he stumbled from the shock and lack of his sword hitting any kind of resistance, Arthur readied his sword again all the same.

The monster whirled around and charged Arthur.

Another burst of light shot out of Bronwyn's chest, hitting the creature's back.

The monster howled in pain, and I resisted the urge to praise Bronwyn. Instead, I gently squeezed her hand.

Uh-oh.

The creature turned in our direction and ran on his smoky legs straight toward . . .

Us.

"What now?" I asked Bronwyn. Admittedly, I was pretty useless at this point, my brain running through any spell I could think of to cast but coming up blank.

Bronwyn didn't answer with words; she shot another beam of light at the monster. It lifted him from the ground and threw him against the wall. The smoke dissipated slightly, the only indication that she might be genuinely hurting it.

Her grip on my hand weakened, and her knees wobbled. I caught her before she could fall to the ground.

Khalid, sword drawn, reached her other side and used his free hand to help her keep her balance.

"You're using too much of your power at once. Let me help you." Back in Avalon, I would never have thought those words would have left my mouth. But I found that my heart ached seeing her so weak after trying to save all our lives from this creature.

Bronwyn's voice shook with fear. "It's so powerful."

My head swung around to see if Merlin was awake yet, as we desperately needed more help, but he was still unconscious. Houdain, having not been able to rein Arthur in, had run over to Merlin and was gently shaking him, obviously hoping for the same thing.

The monster recovered and reformed, then charged toward us again.

"We have to do this, Bronwyn. We're it. Just you and me."

The commotion brought in five of Arthur's knights, and my heart squeezed in fear that they'd be killed within minutes. The flush of terror raced through me as I immediately thought Khalid would race to help them, but he stayed firm by our side. His beautiful brown eyes met mine. "I will never leave you."

My knees wobbled, and not because of the storm monster.

Arthur's knights stood directly in the monster's path, trying desperately to fight him, but their swords passed through the smoke easily, as Arthur's had.

It was enough to anger the creature, or at least enough to provoke him to fight back. The tiny lightning bolts circling around the monster gathered together to form an enormous lightning bolt, which he threw at Arthur's knights. With a loud cracking noise, the knights flew back from the impact of the lightning, slamming against the wall and sliding to the floor, unconscious.

At least I hoped they were unconscious and not *dead*.

As if feeding off the monster's success, Mordred finally showed himself, striding into the great hall with an air of arrogance and satisfaction.

Arthur stepped out into the open, and his face was burdened with hurt and pain. "Mordred." His voice was barely a whisper over the noise of the creature, but everyone heard it.

Mordred turned to Arthur and stared at him with such burning hatred that I almost wanted to avert my gaze. Then Mordred pointed at Arthur, his hand creating tiny lightning bolts that sparked and crawled up his arm. "Destroy!"

"No!" Bronwyn yelled, her voice stronger. She shot out another beam of light, which hit the monster full force in the back.

This time both Mordred and the monster screamed in pain.

Arthur didn't hesitate. He took his window of opportunity and charged Mordred with his sword drawn. As Arthur's sword swung down to end his son's life, Mordred unsheathed his sword and blocked Arthur's attack.

I couldn't focus on them, though, as Bronwyn dropped to her knees. Khalid and I dropped with her, trying to offer support. My stomach twisted in fear and worry. I may have had my issues with Bronwyn, but I realized in that moment that I cared for her deeply. I needed to help her.

Khalid's expression of worry mirrored my own. "What should we do?" he asked.

I didn't know.

My mind was blank.

What spell could we use?

How could we stop this thing?

Now that the creature had recovered enough from Bronwyn's magic, he lumbered toward us at a much slower pace than before. His objective may have been Arthur, but he'd obviously decided he needed to eliminate the threat to his own life first.

"Your blasts only slow it. They're not enough to kill it," I said, instantly receiving a glare from Bronwyn.

"Since I'm the only one hurting it, I suggest you tone down the criticism."

"I'm not criticizing." I genuinely meant it. "I'm terrified, and it's almost here!"

The creature appeared to be gaining strength as it shambled forward.

Bronwyn stared at me with desperate eyes. "Anna, listen to me. You're the spellcaster. You need to come up with a spell. I can give you all the strength I have left, but incantations are not my strength. They're yours."

I knew what it must have taken for her to say that to me, but the truth was . . .

I couldn't think of a single spell.

Sword ready, Khalid stood in front of us. "Priestess Anna, I will give you the time you need to think."

Oh Goddess. The man I loved was risking death to give me time? I couldn't let that happen. I couldn't stop it either.

Charging toward the creature, Khalid let out a battle cry and aimed his blade directly toward a crawling bolt of lightning.

It hit.

It barely hurt the monster, but it did cause it to slow down.

Think, Anna. Think.

Why was my brain being so stubborn?

Khalid took another swing, striking another bolt. From the shake of his arms, my heart wrenched, realizing his body was taking in some of the electric shock of his blows.

Bronwyn forced me to make eye contact with her. "Anna. You

can do this. It's why we were bound. We may not like each other at times, but we are priestesses of Avalon, and we are destined to lead our sisters in the future." Then she swallowed hard. "I believe in you."

Hearing those words filled me with confidence.

An idea struck me.

"The prison spell. The one that kept the mist creature from attacking Avalon a year ago. Priestess Elaine taught it to us in class. If I recite it and you push in that beautiful beam of yours, we could trap it."

Bronwyn's hand squeezed mine tighter. "Let's do it."

We both stood up.

Goddess, don't let me mess this up!

I began reciting the words, and the pulsing I had experienced before from Bronwyn pushed through my hand and up my arm. My goddess, this girl was strong. If a giant storm monster hadn't been beating up my boyfriend to try and murder us, I would've been more terrified than I was. But in this case, it was a strength that only inspired me to hold up my end of the bargain.

I recited the spell over and over, and a small ball of light began to form inside Bronwyn's chest. My words became more steady, more powerful. And the more I repeated them, the bigger the ball of light became until it was almost erupting from Bronwyn's chest.

"Now!" she commanded.

I yelled the last words of the spell as the ball of light burst from Bronwyn and smashed into the storm monster full force.

The creature screamed and writhed as the light surrounded him, encasing him in our joint magic. The tiny lightning bolts that traveled around its body snapped against the light barrier we'd created. Arthur and Mordred stopped their fighting amidst the commotion, watching as the monster appeared to be suffocating inside our spell. We weren't trapping him, we were *killing* him.

Good.

Boom!

It was gone.

All that remained was a glowing afterimage of light, which then dissipated before our eyes.

I quickly glanced at Mordred, wondering if he had enough power to bring it back. But he stared at me with widened, hate-filled eyes, and I knew from the turn of my gut that we had made a dangerous enemy.

Arthur took only seconds to recover, turning on his son, sword raised, ready to strike him down.

But Mordred was gone.

He disappeared as suddenly as the storm monster.

Arthur didn't hesitate, calling for his waking guards to find his son at any cost.

Before I could truly comprehend the chaos, Khalid was by my side, staring at me with those beautiful eyes that made me want to collapse all over again. He leaned down to kiss me, then stopped himself.

We couldn't.

Not with witnesses.

The weight in my chest made it difficult to breathe.

"Are you well, Priestess Anna? Do you need to lie down?"

Bronwyn, though weakened, seemed to be recovering fast as she barked a laugh. "I'll bet she wants to lie down."

I yanked my hand away from hers. "Sh!"

"Sorry," she said, though the smile she gave us was one of genuine happiness.

I smiled back. "Why don't you go see if Houdain needs any help with Merlin? It seems his master is waking up. I'm pretty sure our binding spell will let you go that far."

Bronwyn's smile turned lopsided. "Of course. I'll just leave you two alone."

Before she left, I touched her arm gently. "We did it."

She reached up and touched my hand with genuine affection. "Maybe Priestesses Elaine and Florette knew what they were doing after all."

Before I could respond, Bronwyn walked away toward Houdain and Merlin, and in that moment, I knew that it may be a hard road, but we were going to come out of it better people.

I turned back to Khalid, and though we couldn't show our affection for each other, he wrapped his arm around my waist. "If you're too tired to walk, I can support you."

Smiling up at him knowingly, I placed my arm around his waist as well. "I appreciate it."

Yank!

I nearly fell to my knees. In the distance, Bronwyn laughed and gave me a small wave.

Well, maybe only *one* of us would become a better person.

Chapter 16
BRONWYN

By the time I woke, the sun was already high in the sky. It was as if the storm had never existed.

Anna placed her hands on her hips. "Hurry up. We already missed breakfast, and I'm starving. I hate missing breakfast."

I knew exactly what Anna was like when she missed breakfast. It was ugly.

The extra sleep was good. If I hadn't been there and experienced for myself the exhaustion that came from using almost all my energy to cast spells, I would've felt like it hadn't happened at all.

When we were ready to head out of our room, there was a knock on our doors.

Anna opened them to reveal an adorably disheveled Houdain, who gave a quick wave. "Good morning, priestesses!" Houdain said.

I approached the doors, and he smiled when our eyes met. Oh, the smile!

"Wow! You've got great timing," Anna replied. "We were going to find something to eat."

"Perfect," Houdain said. "Lunch is being served in Master Merlin's apartments. They're waiting for you."

Anna asked, "Who are *they*?"

"Master Merlin and King Arthur."

"Are we in trouble?" That came out of my mouth unexpectedly.

"What? No! Of course not," he said. "You saved the king's life."

"Why would you think we're in trouble?" Anna said, turning around to stare at me. She was clearly annoyed.

"Don't give me that look," I said to Anna. "You know what private meetings with adults usually mean."

Anna's expression softened. "Not if there's a meal involved."

She was right. Why would they want to have lunch with us if they were angry?

Anna stepped into the hallway and fell in line with Khalid (who had arrived from seemingly nowhere, as usual), and I walked behind her with Houdain. I couldn't look at him. First he had risked his life to save mine with Sir Gawain, then he had done it again to help save Arthur. He wasn't even a knight.

"You saved my life," he said, shuffling his feet.

"You tried to save mine with Sir Gawain." *Tried? Way to rub it in!* I was the worst.

Houdain chuckled quietly, then nodded. "I owe you."

"You don't."

"I do."

"You don't."

"Yes, I do!"

"Houdain—"

"It's a code!"

"A code."

"Yes!"

"Well then, we're even because you really were trying to save my life."

"Yeah, but you *actually* saved mine."

"Priestess Elaine says it's the effort that counts."

"Not when it comes to codes."

"That's ridiculous!"

"Tell that to King Arthur."

"Maybe I will!"

"I dare you."

Anna coughed loudly to get my attention. I suddenly noticed we had stopped walking and were standing in front of the doors to Merlin's apartments.

Anna covered her mouth, hiding a grin, one eyebrow arched. Khalid bit his lower lip and stood at attention next to her.

I also noticed that Houdain and I faced each other, our faces inches apart.

Houdain swallowed hard. "Ah. Here we are." He turned away and opened the doors. He waved his hand for us to enter.

Anna stepped beside me, and we headed inside. She whispered, "I thought for sure you guys were going to kiss."

"He'd never kiss me," I hissed.

Anna nearly snorted. "Don't be stupid, Bronwyn."

"I'm not."

"When it comes to love you are, and this is coming from a complete dolt."

Rather than discuss it further, I walked toward the dining area with a slightly faster pace than Anna's. She quickly caught up, smiling at me like a cat who'd swallowed a canary.

King Arthur, Queen Guinevere, and Merlin waited for us at a long wooden table, seated on benches. Merlin wasn't one for fancy furniture or decorations, which reminded me of home. It filled me with a calming warmth as I sat down at the end of the table with Anna, Khalid, and Houdain. The first course of roasted pork and tomatoes was served immediately after we sat. Conversation was polite. The weather was turning again. More invasions in the north. It was terribly boring. At least the food was incredible, as always. I tried to pay attention to what everyone was saying but could only stay awake by focusing on each wonderful bite of food.

As the last plates were taken away, King Arthur interlaced his fingers and put his hands on the table. His gaze shifted back and forth between Anna and me. "I apologize, priestesses. Apparently, Mordred has been trying to kill me for some time."

"I'm sorry." I wasn't sure what else to say. How could you comfort a father whose son was trying to kill him?

The king's face was soft and calm. "I'm still trying to wrap my head around it. I trusted him with my life. He's so powerful . . . I had no idea." Arthur tried to hide what he was feeling from us, but I'd seen it before in my parents when they sent me to Avalon. He was broken.

"Mordred will keep trying," Merlin said. "For now, he's gone far from here."

King Arthur continued after gathering himself back together. "You both fought bravely and intelligently against that monster . . . and Mordred. We are honored to have you call Camelot your home away from Avalon and continue your training."

I let out a breath from relief and pride. From Anna's shoulders relaxing and the smile growing on her face, I could tell she was feeling the same way.

"Thank you, sire," she said.

"Yeah . . . yes, sire. Thank you very much."

Smooth.

"Merlin and I agree that you two should become reacquainted with the Britain that exists today. You should understand the culture and politics of each realm and even beyond, across the seas. You must be well-informed in order to serve Britain as well as Avalon."

"Does that mean we'll be traveling? I've hardly ever traveled!" I blurted out with excitement. I grinned broadly and clapped my hands. Goddess, I was such a peasant!

At least I humored Houdain.

King Arthur smiled at me as if I were his beloved child. "I'm glad to know you like our idea, Priestess Bronwyn. Yes, you two will be traveling across Britain, letting the people put a face to Avalon."

"I think it's a wonderful plan, my lord!" Anna said.

"Good," the high king said. "I was thinking your first excursion would be helping my cousin on her quest."

Quest? I was already in! My whole being fluttered with anticipation.

Of course, we said yes. It sounded exciting, though the details were sparse. We were to help his cousin find some kind of legendary item said to have killed a man called Jesus, whom the Christians revered. Merlin promised to give us more details as we were excused from the dining table.

Houdain escorted Anna and me—Khalid had all but vanished into the fortress walls yet again—back to our room. Tomorrow would be more training and preparations for our first quest. I wanted to invite Houdain in for a game, but Anna reminded me that we needed to check in with High Priestesses Florette and

Elaine.

Once settled in, and after Anna and Khalid had a few minutes of "private time," Anna and I set up our mirror and waited for the high priestesses to appear.

They were happy to see us. Elaine gave us all the gossip, and Florette went over our lessons with Merlin so far. Then she got serious. "Based on what has happened at Camelot, we want to make sure you both understand that High Priestess Elaine and I had no idea how dangerous the world had become. You will work harder with Merlin and also receive nonmagical combat training from Khalid beginning tomorrow."

"High Priestess Florette," Anna began, "you sound . . . frightened."

"I am, Priestess Anna. For you and Bronwyn. Imagine! Merlin needed help from priestesses-in-training against the son of the high king of Britain. Who trained Mordred in magic? Is he as powerful or more powerful than his master? And who or what else could be out there to challenge the greatest magician?" High Priestess Florette took a breath to remain calm. "We are all blessed that you two are quite powerful. But we thought that . . ." Florette cleared her throat, flustered.

"We thought you'd have more time to train and not worry about these things," High Priestess Elaine said. "And thank the Goddess Khalid is with you. He should never leave your sides."

I glanced over at Anna, whose expression was . . . well, it was like stone. Was she going to tell them about her and Khalid?

"What is it, Bronwyn?" High Priestess Elaine asked.

"Huh?"

"What is that look on your face?"

"On *my* face?"

"Yes. You looked at Priestess Anna and then . . ." High Priestess Elaine shook her head and shrugged. "Speak."

My face grew warm as my focus shifted from the high priestesses in the mirror to Anna and back again. I couldn't tell them about Anna and Khalid. I had promised them I wouldn't. Anna and I might still bicker and annoy each other, but after everything we'd been through, she was my sister. I wasn't about to burn everything down by betraying her more than my facial expression already had.

Think, Bronwyn!

"I . . . have no idea what you're talking about."

"I do," Anna whispered.

"What was that, Priestess Anna?" High Priestess Elaine asked, leaning toward their mirror.

I screamed at Anna in my head, *Don't say anything!*

But she either didn't hear or ignored me completely.

"I do," she repeated.

I couldn't let her throw herself to the lions, so I blurted out the first thing that came to my mind. "I have a crush on Merlin's apprentice!" My face grew warm again.

"Oh?" High Priestess Elaine said.

"That's not it," Anna said. "I'm . . . I'm in love . . . with Khalid."

The high priestesses sat back as if they were one person and stared at each other for what seemed like eternity.

"I'm so sorry," I mouthed to Anna, who shook her head at me slowly. She didn't blame me. She wasn't angry. Finally, they returned their attention to us.

High Priestess Florette spoke. "It is forbidden for Avalon guards to be with priestesses, even ones in training."

Anna swallowed hard. The pain in her eyes twisted my stomach.

High Priestess Florette continued. "As long as you can live

with that and do nothing about it, Khalid may remain your guard. That may prove quite difficult. I know from experience."

Anna didn't seem to comprehend the high priestess's words as she fought back tears. My heart hurt for her. But I *was* surprised to hear the high priestess imply that she'd been in love with a guard before. Love in the life of a high priestess of Avalon wasn't very common, and there wasn't much time for it while in training. I was dying to find out what had happened, and a part of me hoped if High Priestess Florette was willing to share, it might help Anna in some way.

"What happened?" I asked.

"I did what I had to do, as did the guard," she said. Her voice softened. "As will you and Khalid. Understood?"

Well, that had backfired.

Anna stood facing the mirror with her head down and eyes closed, tears streaming down her cheeks. Her shaking hands were clenched into fists behind her back.

"Understood, Priestess Anna?" High Priestess Florette repeated.

Anna nodded.

"You both stood bravely in the face of danger," High Priestess Florette said after a deep breath. "Merlin believes you represented Avalon to the highest standards and that word is quickly spreading across Britain about the priestesses of Avalon at the high king's court. You both should be proud. You make a strong team together, in spite of your differences."

"Or perhaps because of them," High Priestess Elaine said with a smile.

High Priestess Florette waggled a finger in a small yet strange pattern and incanted a spell. "In return for your exemplary performance, we have given you both some extra space."

"We'll check in on you again once you have set out on your journey with King Arthur's cousin," High Priestess Elaine said.

They vanished from the mirror.

I faced Anna. "I'm so, so sorry—"

"Thank you, Bronwyn, for trying to cover for me."

"What are you going to do? Can I do anything?"

Anna shook her head. She stood there a moment and then straightened up. She took a deep breath. "I don't know. I mean, I know I want to become a high priestess of Avalon someday, but my feelings for Khalid . . . I just don't know. Try not to let me do anything stupid."

"Would that be your definition of stupid or mine?"

Tears streamed down her cheeks. "Forget it."

"No, no, no. I was kidding. Partially. Hey, High Priestess Florette said they gave us extra space." I grinned at Anna as I took a step backward and then another. Anna and I slowly backed away from each other. She opened the door to the bedroom we'd been unable to use because of our bond. With each step, my excitement grew. I stood at the window of our shared room, and Anna stood at the bed in the second unused room. Anna had made it just past the four-poster frame when my body tugged forward. We stared at each other for a moment. We were about twenty steps apart.

Privacy.

"Privacy!" we yelled together.

I jumped onto our shared bed, and Anna jumped onto the bed in the other room.

With a spring to her step, Anna joined me on our bed, and we jumped a few times together. We both collapsed onto the soft mattress with a laugh.

Anna said, "I can't believe you admitted having a crush on Houdain."

"I said that to save your butt."

"Doesn't mean it's not true."

"It doesn't matter."

"What are you talking about? It's important."

"It's not, Anna. It's a dumb one-way crush."

Anna paused and softened her expression. "It's not one-way. Houdain really likes you."

I threw a pillow at Anna, and she ducked. She giggled as she returned to the new room. She was just trying to embarrass me. It didn't work. I knew full well if Houdain did have a crush on me, it would fade the longer he'd get to know the *real* me.

Apart but together. Together apart. Clearly, Anna and I had a long way to go if we were going to be a strong pair of high priestesses. But we had worked together enough to defeat a monster, scare off a powerful magician, save the high king of Britain, and impress the greatest wizard of all and, most importantly, High Priestesses Florette and Elaine.

My body ached in exhaustion, though it was barely midday. I tried to imagine Anna and me, older and hopefully wiser, sitting beside an ancient King Arthur. But every time the image sharpened, it was replaced by a curtain of red light. Was it a sign? Was our future as high priestesses of Avalon in doubt?

To calm my mind, I thought about that timeless space where I'd met Merlin, and it filled me with a warm glow. I wanted to learn how to get there on my own. As I drifted to sleep, I continued to visualize that place, and for a moment, I thought I heard Merlin's voice, but it was distant and filled with echoes.

I concentrated harder, using all my energy to hear his words.

Finally, after what seemed like hours, though it could only have been a moment, his voice sharpened, clear and loud.

"Spear of Destiny."

A chill ran down my back.

What were we getting into?

Other Books

By Marni L.B. Troop

Tir Na N'Og Saga
Tir Na N'Og: Journal One
The Heart of Ireland: Journal Two

By Becca C. Smith

The Riser Saga:
Riser

Reaper

Ripper

The Atlas Series:
Atlas

Grigori Returned

The Underworld

Riser Saga/Atlas Series Finale:
Atlas Rising

The Dream Diaries:
The Dream Diaries

The Dream Diaries: Blood Ties

Jeraline's Alley

Alexis Tappendorf Series:
Alexis Tappendorf and the Search for Beale's Treasure

Alexis Tappendorf and the Search for Atlantis

Love & Dark Series (with Hina McCord):
Vessel

First Born

Gutian Code

BIOGRAPHIES

Becca

Becca fell in love with storytelling at an early age. The first book she read was The Lion, The Witch and The Wardrobe and she's been looking for the door to Narnia ever since! Becca is a passionate reader, consuming anything sci-fi or fantasy. Mix it in with YA and she is a fan for life. So it's no surprise that she writes in these genres as well. When Becca isn't writing, she loves to sew. From Mortal Instruments rune pillows, to elaborate Firefly/Serenity bags, Becca loves to create!

Marni

When Marni was in college, she had the opportunity to visit Ireland. Having fallen in love with the country, its people and its mythology, she spent the better part of twenty years researching Irish Celtic history, folklore and literature.

Marni has taught literature, rhetoric and composition at the college level since 1997. Since 1993, she has worked in and around the film and television industry in Los Angeles as a ghost writer for independent filmmakers, a script and novel editor and a story analyst for production companies.

One of her poems was published in a Welch anthology of American poetry.

Marni holds a Masters in Professional Writing from the University of Southern California.